NOT ON MY BOTCH

THE WORST DETECTIVE EVER, BOOK 11

CHRISTY BARRITT

COMPLETE BOOK LIST

Squeaky Clean Mysteries:
#1 Hazardous Duty
#2 Suspicious Minds
#2.5 It Came Upon a Midnight Crime (novella)
#3 Organized Grime
#4 Dirty Deeds
#5 The Scum of All Fears
#6 To Love, Honor and Perish
#7 Mucky Streak
#8 Foul Play
#9 Broom & Gloom
#10 Dust and Obey
#11 Thrill Squeaker
#11.5 Swept Away (novella)
#12 Cunning Attractions
#13 Cold Case: Clean Getaway

#14 Cold Case: Clean Sweep

#15 Cold Case: Clean Break

#16 Cleans to an End

While You Were Sweeping, A Riley Thomas Spinoff

The Sierra Files:

#1 Pounced

#2 Hunted

#3 Pranced

#4 Rattled

The Gabby St. Claire Diaries (a Tween Mystery series):

#1 The Curtain Call Caper

#2 The Disappearing Dog Dilemma

#3 The Bungled Bike Burglaries

The Worst Detective Ever

#1 Ready to Fumble

#2 Reign of Error

#3 Safety in Blunders

#4 Join the Flub

#5 Blooper Freak

#6 Flaw Abiding Citizen

#7 Gaffe Out Loud

#8 Joke and Dagger

#9 Wreck the Halls

#10 Glitch and Famous

#11 Not on My Botch

Raven Remington

Relentless

Holly Anna Paladin Mysteries:

#1 Random Acts of Murder

#2 Random Acts of Deceit

#2.5 Random Acts of Scrooge

#3 Random Acts of Malice

#4 Random Acts of Greed

#5 Random Acts of Fraud

#6 Random Acts of Outrage

#7 Random Acts of Iniquity

Lantern Beach Mysteries

#1 Hidden Currents

#2 Flood Watch

#3 Storm Surge

#4 Dangerous Waters

#5 Perilous Riptide

#6 Deadly Undertow

Lantern Beach Romantic Suspense

#1 Tides of Deception

Lantern Beach Blackout: The New Recruits

#1 Rocco

#2 Axel

#3 Beckett

#4 Gabe

Lantern Beach Mayday

#1 Run Aground

#2 Dead Reckoning

#3 Tipping Point

Lantern Beach Blackout: Danger Rising

#1 Brandon

#2 Dylan

#3 Maddox

#4 Titus

Lantern Beach Christmas

Silent Night

Crime á la Mode

#1 Dead Man's Float

#2 Milkshake Up

#3 Bomb Pop Threat

#4 Banana Split Personalities

Beach Bound Books and Beans Mysteries

#1 Bound by Murder

#2 Bound by Disaster

#3 Bound by Mystery

#4 Bound by Trouble

#5 Bound by Mayhem

Vanishing Ranch

#1 Forgotten Secrets

#2 Necessary Risk

#3 Risky Ambition

#4 Deadly Intent

#5 Lethal Betrayal

#6 High Stakes Deception

#7 Fatal Vendetta

#8 Troubled Tidings

#9 Narrow Escape

The Sidekick's Survival Guide

#1 The Art of Eavesdropping

#2 The Perks of Meddling

#3 The Exercise of Interfering

#4 The Practice of Prying

#5 The Skill of Snooping

#6 The Craft of Being Covert

Saltwater Cowboys

#1 Saltwater Cowboy

#2 Breakwater Protector

#3 Cape Corral Keeper

#4 Seagrass Secrets

#5 Driftwood Danger

#6 Unwavering Security

Beach House Mysteries

#1 The Cottage on Ghost Lane

#2 The Inn on Hanging Hill

#3 The House on Dagger Point

School of Hard Rocks Mysteries

#1 The Treble with Murder

#2 Crime Strikes a Chord

#3 Tone Death

Carolina Moon Series

#1 Home Before Dark

#2 Gone By Dark

#3 Wait Until Dark

#4 Light the Dark

#5 Taken By Dark

Suburban Sleuth Mysteries:

Death of the Couch Potato's Wife

Fog Lake Suspense:

#1 Edge of Peril

#2 Margin of Error

#3 Brink of Danger

#4 Line of Duty

#5 Legacy of Lies

#6 Secrets of Shame

#7 Refuge of Redemption

Cape Thomas Series:

#1 Dubiosity

#2 Disillusioned

#3 Distorted

Standalone Romantic Mystery:

The Good Girl

Suspense:

Imperfect

The Wrecking

Sweet Christmas Novella:

Home to Chestnut Grove

Standalone Romantic-Suspense:

Keeping Guard

The Last Target

Race Against Time

Ricochet

Key Witness

Lifeline

High-Stakes Holiday Reunion

Desperate Measures

Hidden Agenda

Mountain Hideaway

Dark Harbor

Shadow of Suspicion

The Baby Assignment

The Cradle Conspiracy

Trained to Defend

Mountain Survival

Dangerous Mountain Rescue

Nonfiction:

Characters in the Kitchen

Changed: True Stories of Finding God through Christian Music (out of print)

The Novel in Me: The Beginner's Guide to Writing and Publishing a Novel (out of print)

"JOEY, why in the world are you at the grocery store? I thought you were meeting us for lunch." Dizzy Jenkins' voice came through my cell phone sounding high-pitched and almost accusatory—in the most loving way possible, of course.

But she wasn't making any sense. Why would she think I wasn't meeting her and the rest of the Hot Chicks?

I stared out my car window at the causeway in front of me, one that stretched across the Roanoke Sound between Nags Head and Roanoke Island, North Carolina. "What do you mean? I'm not at the grocery store. I'm on the way to meet you. You know I don't cook, right? And I have my groceries delivered!"

"I'm just telling you what I'm seeing on social

media. Maxine has it on her phone now, and we're all watching. It's one of those on-time videos."

I pressed the brakes as a tourist laden with a surfboard, a bright-orange innertube, and a cooler nearly lost his balance and stepped into traffic. "You mean real time? A real-time video?"

"Yes, real time. Anyway, according to social media, you're at The Fresh Grocer right now. I'm watching you with my own eyes."

"Wait . . . The Fresh Grocer . . . is this a joke?" Dizzy could be *so* inappropriate sometimes. But it was *hysterical.*

I seriously had no idea what my aunt was talking about.

I gripped my steering wheel, about to turn into the parking lot at The Fatty Shack so I could meet Dizzy and the other Hot Chicks for lunch.

The Hot Chicks were four widows who'd formed a late-in-life clique. At times, it seemed as if I were an unofficial member—even though I wasn't a widow and was thirty years their junior. Still, they never failed to entertain me with their antics.

Gregarious Dizzy was my aunt by marriage and a hairdresser who owned Beach Combers salon.

Strong-willed Maxine owned Utter Clutter, a store that sold fabulously repurposed furniture.

Level-headed Geraldine had been a homemaker.

Sweet MaryAnn was a retired teacher.

"I have no idea what you're talking about," I repeated as I put my red Miata into Park. "Send me a link."

Now I was curious.

"All right," Dizzy muttered. "We're sending it now."

I ended my call with her and watched as the link appeared. I clicked on it as compulsively as a gambling addict playing the slots.

Sure enough, a video of me outside a grocery store signing autographs filled the screen.

The problem was the person in the video wasn't me.

I squinted as I watched.

It was strange because the person *did* look like me. As in *just* like me. This woman even moved like me.

What in the world was going on?

I stared at the video another moment before throwing my car back into Drive.

I needed to see this with my own eyes. The Fresh Grocer was only five minutes away. What better way to find some answers than by addressing this issue head-on. Surely, there was some type of explanation for what was happening . . . though I couldn't fathom what.

A clone? A movie stunt by my publicist? An extravagant practical joke?

I pulled up at the back of the lot at The Fresh Grocer and parked.

I didn't have to get out to see what the hubbub was about. A crowd had formed near the entrance with their phones raised.

I held back a touch of envy.

There were times my stardom got me some attention. But for the most part, I went on with life as a normal person. Because that's what I was—a normal person. And that's what I wanted—to have a normal life.

So how had some Joey Darling impersonator managed to get all this attention at a grocery store? It wasn't like we were in Hollywood or at a red-carpet premier.

I almost got out, but I didn't. Instead, I watched. Then I pulled out my own phone.

I wanted to send my husband—police detective Jackson Sullivan—a video of this, just in case. This could be a matter of him getting a good laugh.

Or there could be something more sinister going on.

I was the type who just happened to see mystery and suspense in everything . . . and right now I was getting major *Single White Female* vibes.

As the crowd cleared, I saw myself.

Or I saw the person who looked like me, I should say.

She wore jean shorts, a fuchsia top, and black Converse. Her long, dark hair flowed over her shoulders, and a bright, wide grin stretched across her face.

I cracked my window enough to hear her say, "I'm sorry, but now I really need to get back to grocery shopping. I have a hot date with my husband tonight, and I need to cook him something fabulous."

Lies! I'd never say something like that.

With a wink and a confident wave, the woman sauntered inside the store, and the crowd around her dispersed.

I frowned.

Hmmm . . . how interesting.

Should I confront this woman? I mean, she *was* purposely pretending to be me.

I wasn't sure what to do. As a celebrity, I'd seen and experienced a lot of crazy things—fans breaking into my house, following me into public bathrooms to ask for my autograph under the stall, and a man who'd once told me that I was the mother of his two-year-old child.

But never this.

And now, as the man in black from *The Princess*

Bride would say, I'd come to an impasse.

Should I confront her? Or leave?

The choice seemed . . . inconceivable.

I pulled my baseball hat lower and threw on some sunglasses—I always kept both handy for times like this.

Of *course* I wasn't leaving.

No, I was going to sneak into the store.

I had to get a closer look. Some people let their emotions lead them.

Me? My curiosity dictated my actions and had gotten me into scrapes on more than one occasion. Now snooping just seemed like part of my life.

I grabbed a cart near the entrance and kept my head low so no one would pay any attention to me.

Then I wandered into the store, scanning the aisles for my look-alike.

Finally, I spotted the woman heading toward the back of the store.

As she reached the doors leading into the Employee Only area, she paused and glanced around.

I quickly slipped behind a display of night-crawlers.

Yes, even the biggest grocery stores in this ocean-side town stocked fishing worms.

I remained hunched until I heard a footstep.

Then this woman disappeared into the back of the store.

Now I was more curious than ever.

I glanced around again, making sure no one was watching. The vacationers around me seemed too busy filling their carts to overflowing to pay attention.

I paused by the Employees Only area—but only for a moment.

Then I pushed through the heavy rubber doors and listened to them sweep across the concrete below.

Two employees worked in the storage area, but they didn't notice me.

Who I didn't see, however, was my clone.

Remaining along the wall, I crept toward an office.

It was empty.

Then I crept toward a back exit that had been left open a mere crack.

I peered out.

There she was!

Meeting with a man behind the store. The guy wore all black, including a black baseball cap that shadowed his features. From what I could tell, he was maybe in his thirties, and his bulging muscles showed his strength.

Something in my gut told me to stay out of sight.

So I did.

"Did you get it?" the man asked.

"Not yet," the woman said, her voice nearly a whisper. "I'm trying."

"Try harder!" The man sounded demanding as he leered at her.

"It's not as easy as you might think. I don't know what else I can do!"

"You have three days to come up with something. Understand?"

She nodded. "Of course."

"Take this with you." He handed her an envelope, which she quickly tucked into her pocket.

As the man shifted, the black button-up shirt he wore over his T-shirt moved.

I sucked in a breath.

A gun was holstered around his shoulders.

What was going on here?

No way would I confront them now. Not with a weapon involved.

But I was more curious than ever as to who this woman was, what she was up to, and why she was impersonating me.

CHAPTER
TWO

"SOMEONE IS IMPERSONATING YOU?" Jackson repeated as I drove down the road.

I had him on speaker so we could talk.

"Isn't that crazy?" I muttered, fighting irritation as traffic thickened.

In the winter, I could zip through this area in no time.

In the summer? Thousands of people visited the island and clogged the streets.

I didn't mind tourists—I wasn't a local myself, after all. But I wished the town's infrastructure could go all Antman in certain seasons and quadruple in size, only to shrink again in the off-season.

"Does that mean you've reached another layer of stardom?" Jackson asked with a chuckle. "Like Elvis? Before you know it, there will be Joey Darling impersonators having contests all over the country. Drinking smoothies and Izzes. Doing the baloney move."

"Ha ha. Very funny. I just don't know whether I should be flattered or concerned."

"For now, how about flattered?"

I remembered the sketchy scene at the back of the grocery store. Something about it concerned me, but I couldn't put my finger on what.

Well, besides the gun beneath the guy's shirt.

That *definitely* concerned me.

Should I mention what I saw? I hadn't described that part of the story to Jackson yet.

I wasn't sure. If there was one thing I'd learned, it was that I couldn't be the girl who cried wolf. Nope. I had to know for sure before I mentioned any potential crimes. I would no longer overreact.

"There's more," I started.

I should definitely tell him.

"Hold that thought," Jackson said. "I've got a call I have to take. Can we talk about this later?"

"Of course. You'll be home for dinner tonight, right? I can make . . . salad." Like I'd reminded Dizzy, I didn't really cook.

"I should be. And pull out a steak to defrost for me, please."

I grinned as I stared at the road ahead of me. "Perfect. I can't wait to see you."

I had visions of a nice cookout on our back deck tonight. We could catch up and do ordinary types of things. No investigating or anything else that could lead to trouble and upset the new norm I'd established as a mature married woman.

"Love you, Joey."

"Love you too, husband." I smiled as I said the word.

I still couldn't believe Jackson and I were married.

Two blissful months had passed since we tied the knot and went on our honeymoon to St. Barts. I still had another five weeks until I began filming again. My last movie, *Family Secrets*, had done exceedingly well. And *Relentless*, my TV show, had wrapped up its newest season and wouldn't start filming again until the fall.

Talk about a whirlwind.

I was still learning all the ins and outs of being a wife. Since my own mother had left when I was too young to remember, I didn't exactly have a good example to follow.

For so long, it had just been me and my dad.

But now he was gone . . .

I frowned at the thought.

He wasn't *gone* gone. He'd simply disappeared

for a while because of some danger that had arisen in his life—thanks to my mom—although I hesitated to even call the woman that.

She'd abandoned me and my dad when I was six months old and had only reappeared last year to wreak havoc in my life.

I ended the call with Jackson and focused on driving back to The Fatty Shack. Dizzy and the ladies were still waiting for me there.

In just a couple of minutes, I pulled into the parking lot.

The restaurant had been established before tourism had taken over the island, and this was still where locals liked to eat.

The inside looked dated and was decorated with old crab pots and vintage buoys, but it did have a wonderful view of the Roanoke Sound. My signed picture was framed on the wall, and a jukebox in the corner played oldies but goodies.

This had been my dad's favorite place to eat, and I always felt close to him when I was here.

As I stepped inside, the scents of fried seafood and homemade hushpuppies surrounded me.

The Hot Chicks spotted me from across the restaurant and waved me over.

I braced myself to rehash the drama of my impersonator again.

There was no way the ladies would let me off the hook about that video—not until I shared every little detail.

"So . . . what was all of that about?" Dizzy asked as she pushed an extra glass of water she'd ordered toward me.

I ran through what had transpired, and they all listened raptly.

Before I even had a chance to order food—I was talking too much—the waitress placed a stacked bamboo steamer basket in front of me.

Instantly, I salivated.

This dish was my favorite. Each layer of the basket contained a different treat: fresh shrimp, broccoli, zucchini, carrots. Small ramakins of butter and freshly grated parmesan waited on the side.

I usually didn't touch the butter, though. I hated the fact that I was constantly worrying about my weight, but it came with the job.

"That's so strange." MaryAnn picked up half of her seafood wrap. "I wonder exactly what someone is trying to accomplish. I mean, does this woman really want people to think she's you? And if so, why? Does she want to profit from your success somehow? Does she get a thrill from feeling famous?"

"I like the way you're thinking." I nodded slowly. "Psychology is a fascinating subject. I did this movie once where the government created AI doppelgangers for everyone in the Senate—doppelgangers that did horrible things. It was all to cause a psychological impact on voters—"

"*Dead Ringer*." Dizzy did the seal clap—the one where her wrists remained together but her hands moved in a clapping motion—like a seal. "I've seen it three times, and I personally think it's one of your best."

I straightened my shoulders. "Well, thank you."

"Anyway . . ." Dizzy continued. "I think this woman is someone we should *definitely* keep an eye on."

I glanced at everyone at the table as I stabbed a shrimp with my fork. "If you guys see anything else from her online, let me know."

Just as with Jackson, I contemplated whether or not I should tell them about the exchange I'd seen behind the grocery store and the man with the gun. I hadn't gotten that far yet—only to the part where I followed this woman into the Employees Only area.

But the Hot Chicks would react entirely differently to this part of the story than my husband would. Whereas Jackson would tell me to stay out of it, the Hot Chicks would want to jump right into the thick of things with me.

Depending on the day, I liked both of those reactions for different reasons.

I finished my shrimp and speared a piece of broccoli, waving it in the air. "Does this mean I have reached the next level of fame?"

I glanced all around the table.

"You have six million followers on Twitter," Geraldine said. "I'd say you're already there."

"Anyway . . . I know we didn't all get together just so we could talk about my career." I glanced at each lady. "How's everyone doing?"

Everyone began talking, specifically focusing on some new guy who'd moved to town and joined the ROMEOs—Real Old Men Eating Out. I had a feeling Dizzy and Maxine might both be vying for the same man.

In the middle of their stories, my gaze drifted to a man who stepped into the restaurant. A man who almost looked familiar.

He was tall with thick, dark hair and intelligent eyes. His features were sharp but handsome. He wore a white, long-sleeved button-up shirt—one that made him look more suited for an office than The Fatty Shack.

Though he looked familiar, at the same time I was certain I'd never seen him before.

The man glanced around the dining area before spotting me. Then he strode my way and paused at the table.

"Hi, Joey," he started, a touch of hesitation to his voice. "I know you don't know who I am. But I was really hoping that I could have a moment of your time."

I'd been around way too many psychotic fans to say yes to that request. "If you have anything to say to me, you can say it in front of my friends."

He still hesitated as he glanced at the Hot Chicks before connecting his gaze with mine again. "The matter is rather sensitive."

I'd heard *that* before. And I wasn't going to fall for it.

But I'd be lying if I said I wasn't curious. Then again, when was I *not* curious?

"I'm sure whatever you have to say, it's just fine being said right here. You understand I need to be cautious, correct?"

The man swallowed hard before nodding. "If that's the way you want to play this."

Something about the way he said the words made my nerves tighten.

I waited with anticipation.

Finally, he drew in a deep breath, and his gaze connected with mine.

"There's no easy way to say this, so I'm just going to come right out with it." He swallowed so hard that his Adams apple nearly burst from his throat. "Joey, I am your father."

JOEY . . . *I am your father.*

For some reason, in my mind, this man's voice had transformed into Darth Vader's as he said the words.

I quickly snapped from those thoughts, knowing they were silly—silliness was my coping mechanism.

But his statement had been unbelievable.

Both trepidation and curiosity pressed between my shoulders as I stepped outside. I felt the Hot Chicks' lingering glances on me as if they were concerned. But this truly was one conversation I needed to have in private.

I knew if I needed them, the ladies were just one shout away and would run outside with forks—the regular ones from the restaurants since pitchforks weren't readily available—cell phone cameras, and maybe even a can of travel-sized hairspray, which worked just fine in a pinch if you didn't have pepper spray. No doubt, they'd be watching me from the window. I knew them well enough to know that.

The early summer sun felt especially hot as I led the man around the corner and out of range of anyone who might attempt to listen. Or was that some type of internal heat that caused me to sweat?

And why now, of all times, did the marsh in the distance have to smell like rotten eggs? The stench only made this situation worse.

I ignored those thoughts and stared at the man in front of me, wondering if his gaze should be familiar to me. Wondering if his eyes looked like my own.

They *were* the same brown color. Same basic distance apart. Same basic shape.

But I couldn't let that play with my emotions and logic.

This guy could be someone off the street who claimed to be my father in order to get money from me. People assumed I was loaded.

I *was* rather comfortable now that I'd paid much of my debt off and had a relatively steady paycheck coming in. But no one was going to fool me.

Even though it had happened plenty of times in the past . . . but let's not bring that up right now.

I licked my lips before saying, "So . . . you think you're my dad?"

He didn't crack a smile or give any indication he was joking as he nodded. "That's right. I know this is hard for you to hear. And I know you've always thought of Lewis Schermerhorn as your father. The truth is, Lewis doesn't know that he's not really your father."

At the mention of my dad—my real dad—my defenses went up.

I didn't think this guy was telling the truth.

But if he was, then my *dad* dad would be devastated when he heard.

I *definitely* needed more information.

"You need to start explaining." I crossed my arms. "Because right now I don't believe a word you're saying. You could've found out my father's name online. You could've found out I was living in this area through an old interview I did. None of this is making any sense."

He casually rested his hands in the front pockets of his slacks. "I know that this is a lot to comprehend, and I'm sorry to throw it on you like this. But I figured it was best to be blunt and get the facts out there rather than beat around the bush. Many years ago, your mother and I used to work together. Thirty to be exact."

Thirty years ago? How convenient. That would've been exactly one year before I was born. Again, my age and birthdate were something he could've looked up.

"Where did you and my mom work together?" I tried not to give him any additional indications that his story had hints of truth to it. Not yet, at least.

"Your mother and I worked together for the government. She was my asset."

I couldn't help it. I laughed. As the absurdity of all his statements hit me, I laughed harder and harder.

This guy *couldn't* be telling the truth.

I knew my mom was involved with some bad stuff, including a crime ring called the Barracudas.

But an asset? As in the super-secret spy kind of asset?

That was laughable.

"Why are you doing this?" I stared up at the man, searching for the truth in his gaze. "Why are you making this up? Do you just want to make my life more of a headache? Why can't you people leave me alone?"

I started to walk away, and the man grabbed my arm.

I glanced at his fingers as they curled around my bicep and kept staring until he released me. Then I pulled my arm back, hoping the motion indicated that he was never to touch me again.

"I'm not trying to pull one over on you." His voice softened. "I don't want anything from you even. I just wanted you to know the truth. If you think I'm coming after your money or looking for recognition or fame, you're wrong."

I didn't say anything. I only stared.

If he didn't want anything from me, that would be a step in the right direction. However, I didn't trust him. And I didn't trust his statements.

Because he wouldn't have shown up if he didn't want something.

If he was telling the truth then, at the very least, he wanted a relationship of some sort with me, whether it was distant or close. But he wasn't telling the truth, so I took that option off the table.

I narrowed my eyes. "Why now? Just for kicks, let's say your story is true. Why did you wait thirty years to come find me?"

He dropped his gaze as if burdened by the question. "I worked a very covert job filled with danger. I was in no position to be a parent. Apparently, Melinda wasn't either. But I kept watch over you from a distance."

"Melinda?" I tapped my foot.

"That's your mom's real name. Melinda Fischer."

I stored that name away, even though I doubted he was telling the truth.

I'd known her as Laura Schermerhorn from Georgia, the woman who'd left us to pursue a modeling career that never materialized.

She'd introduced herself to me as Anita Briggs when she'd shown up here in town.

And now there was another name?

Somehow, the idea this man might know more about my mother than I did didn't sit well with me.

I wondered momentarily why he looked familiar. If I'd seen him before. Or if he simply looked familiar because we shared common features.

Was this guy really a part of my mom's past?

Or I could be reading entirely too much into this, and this man wasn't related to me at all.

Which was the most likely scenario.

My thoughts jumped all over the place.

"My own father passed away last week, and it made me reevaluate my own life. That's when I decided to come here and find you."

"You're not my father." Defensiveness rose in me. "Nothing you can tell me will make me believe it."

"I know this is a lot to comprehend." He pressed something into my hand. "This is my number. I'll be in town for the rest of the week if you want to talk more."

I glanced at the card he'd given me. It didn't have a name on it or an address or anything else to indicate anything personal. It was simply ten numbers.

It was such a spy-like thing to give someone a phone number with no name.

I briefly contemplated throwing it into the water or ripping it to shreds or lighting it on fire. The candle on the table inside would do the trick.

Instead, I slipped it into the back pocket of my black jean shorts.

If I changed my mind, there would be plenty of time to destroy this paper later.

I watched the man start to disappear around the corner. "Wait . . . what's your name?"

"Adolf . . ." he called, offering no last name.

Really? Adolf? What a terrible name.

That solidified it. The man was not my father.

My dad couldn't be named Adolf.

As he disappeared, I felt like my world was on the verge of turning upside down.

The Hot Chicks anxiously awaited another update as they munched on an extra basket of hushpuppies at the table.

When I'd started out in showbiz, I thought the

entertaining part of my life would be on-screen. But it turned out my personal life was pretty entertaining also. At least, according to some people it was.

Not that I wanted it to be. But my quest for normal always took detours.

"So?" Dizzy dramatically spread some honey butter over her split hushpuppy. "What kind of con artist is he?"

"He's a good one." I glanced at my cold food.

I'd really been looking forward to eating the rest of that steamer basket.

I went through the conversation with the ladies, hoping I didn't regret sharing these details. I felt like I should tell Jackson first since he was my *husband*.

But the Hot Chicks were here, and I needed a listening ear—or eight.

Besides, Jackson had said he had an important case he was working on, and I didn't want to interrupt him.

I did that enough anyway.

"That man's not your father! Lewis is. I don't know what kind of scheme he's trying to pull." Dizzy scowled and slapped the table.

Our waters quivered in fear, and one of the hushpuppies ran for its life and dove off the side of the table.

Her late husband had been my dad's brother, so Lewis was family to her.

Good family. Close family.

The kind of family you didn't betray.

And acknowledging this other man would be a betrayal.

"To be honest, I don't know anything right now." I shook my head, sensing a headache coming on. "I feel like I just need to go home and decompress while I think this over."

Another part of me wanted to try to track this man down. To find out his real name—it certainly couldn't be Adolf. To discover where he was staying.

Mostly, I wanted to know what he was up to.

And I still might do those things—although it was too late to follow him from the restaurant. That window of opportunity had closed like a barricade over an armory.

But this was big. It was bigger than any mystery a stranger might approach me with. Yes, that happened surprisingly often. People mistook me for the iconic detective I played on TV.

I needed time to figure out how to handle this properly.

Just as I stood, Maxine glanced at her phone and said, "Uh oh."

I didn't like the sound of that.

"What?" I almost didn't want to ask the question.

She held up the device, its bedazzled case glinting in the sunlight. "I just got a notice. I set up a Google alert with your name—not to be creepy, but just because you do want to know these things, right? Anyway, I got a news alert saying you're going to be interviewed on the local news tonight."

"What?" My voice rose. "My publicist didn't say anything to me about that."

I started to check my phone, just to make sure.

"Oh, well . . . it's about living in the Outer Banks. It looks as if the feature has already been recorded because they're showing snippets of the interview."

I gave up on my phone search and stared at Maxine, feeling dumbfounded.

"Let me see that." I didn't mean to, but I snatched her phone.

Then I rewound the video by dragging the little button back across the line at the bottom of the screen. I hit Play and watched the promo for tonight's story.

I sucked in a breath at the clip they showed.

That wasn't me the reporter interviewed.

It was my look-alike.

My muscles hardened.

This woman had just taken things entirely too far.

CHAPTER
FOUR

AS SOON AS I got back to my house, I petted Ripley—our Australian shepherd—and took him on a quick walk.

Then I sat at my kitchen table and opened my laptop to find the contact information for the reporter. We didn't have a local news station, so I couldn't simply pay the woman a visit.

Instead, networks from Hampton Roads, Virginia, sent people down to the Outer Banks—which was part of their viewing area—to cover stories like this.

I'd seen the reporter's name on the news, and I knew I needed to contact her.

Thankfully, the station she worked for advertised her email and phone number on their website in case people had tips.

I dialed her number, and she answered on the first ring.

"Amanda Walters." A perky yet professional voice came over the line.

"Amanda . . . this is Joey Darling."

"Joey! It was so nice to chat with you yesterday. Thank you so much for sitting down with me."

The nerves in my spine seemed to pinch. "That's the thing. I didn't sit down with you."

There was a pause. "What do you mean?"

"I'm telling you that the lady you interviewed was not me."

She paused again. "Is this a joke?"

"It's not a joke. Not at all. You interviewed someone who's pretending to be me."

"Wait, wait, wait . . . she looked and sounded just like you. And she knew all about Hollywood and your shows. Are you sure this isn't a joke?"

"Look, I would talk to you face-to-face right now if I could. But I'm down here in Nags Head, and I'm assuming you're up near Norfolk."

"I am."

"So I hate to do it this way, but it has to be over the phone."

Amanda remained silent a moment before asking, "Can I FaceTime you? I need to see you so I can know I'm not being taken for a ride . . . potentially for a second time."

"Of course. You've got my number. Call me right back."

A few seconds later, she did. Her ebony-colored skin, springy curls, and bright but quickly fading smile stared back at me.

"It *is* you." She shook her head, sounding shocked as she stared. "This *isn't* some kind of prank . . . I thought for sure it might be."

"It's not." I frowned, growing more and more irate over what my look-alike was doing and how far she'd taken it. "I don't want to get my lawyer or manager involved—and, for the record, my manager is *way* scarier than my lawyer—but you can*not* air a story on Joey Darling that features a woman who isn't actually me."

"But it's a great story. You were so—*she* was so— eloquent and interesting." Regret and disappoint- ment saturated her voice.

"I need this woman's contact information. What address did she give you?"

Amanda checked her notes and rattled off the address.

I scowled when I realized I'd jotted my own address on the paper.

My look-alike knew where I lived. Not comforting.

"Phone number?"

This time when Amanda gave me the information, the number wasn't mine. I quickly wrote it down.

"I'm going to need to see a copy of that story," I told her. "In fact, if I could just see all of the camera footage, it would be helpful."

"But—"

I quickly cut her off, not having time to listen to her excuses. "It's one thing if someone wants to look like me. But it's an entirely different story if someone's impersonating me and going live on TV with it."

Amanda paused and then nodded, her voice sounding more subdued when she said, "I understand. I promise you, I had no idea."

"I believe you. She's tricking other people also. But I need to get to the bottom of this. I need that information *now*." I used my best Raven Remington voice as I said the words.

Raven was my alter ego, the character I played on my TV show, *Relentless,* and she was my opposite. Where I was soft, she was hard. Where I was easy, she was tough. Where I had no common sense, she had tons of street smarts.

"Give me your email address, and I'll send it to you right away," Amanda said. "Please, I don't want any trouble. But I'm going to need to go talk to my producer. We've already advertised this story."

I let out a long breath, hating when I had to be the bad guy. But there was no way I was letting her convince me that running the story was a good idea. "You do what you have to do. I'm probably going to have to file a police report, not against you, but against this woman. The cops will probably want to talk to you. I just want to let you know that."

"Of course. It makes sense. I feel so foolish. I've only been on this job for three months and . . ." Amanda pressed her lips together as moisture filled her gaze. She quickly fanned her face as if to dry the tears that wanted to escape.

At once, a touch of the hostility I'd felt toward her disappeared. I knew what it was like to botch things.

I did it all the time, for that matter. So much that I felt like the queen of messing up.

At least, it kept me humble.

"Just send me the videos, and we'll go from there. But if you're telling the truth, then you shouldn't have anything to worry about."

"Okay. I'm sending it now. Keep your eyes open."

I planned on doing just that.

As I stared at my computer screen, my front door opened, and Ripley began to wag his tail.

I jumped to my feet and rounded the corner to see who it was—even though only one other person had a key to the house.

A smile stretched across my face when I spotted Jackson deposit his keys on the table in the entryway.

Handsome Jackson with his barely there beard, muscular—but not *too* muscular—physique, light brown hair, and piercing blue eyes.

In six strides, I met him and threw my arms around him.

He was . . . well, he was my everything and more than I could have ever asked for.

Yes, I'd hit the jackpot. I was pretty sure Jackson felt equally as lucky.

Jackson let out a chuckle. "This is the kind of greeting I could get used to."

I hugged him tighter. After the day I'd had, seeing him was such a welcome relief.

"You'll never believe today," I started as I pulled back.

He planted a quick kiss on my lips before studying my gaze. "What do you mean? I thought you were going to work out, walk Ripley, and then meet the Hot 'Troublemaker' Chicks for lunch."

That's what he'd taken to calling them lately, and I had to admit that the name was fitting.

"I have a feeling that's not the way things worked out," he continued.

I dropped my head to the side and did a half eye roll. "You got here just in time. I want you to watch this with me."

"Watch what?"

"You'll see."

I grabbed my computer from the kitchen and then went to sit on the couch beside him. Ripley jumped beside us, never one to be left out.

When I checked my email, the video was there. I clicked on it and watched as my face filled the screen.

Or my look-alike's face filled the screen, I should say.

Jackson scrubbed his hand over his jaw as if he couldn't believe what he was seeing. "Wait . . . is that the woman impersonating you?"

"She looks a lot like me, doesn't she?"

"There's no way she looks that much like you naturally. Did she have surgery or something?"

Another thought slammed into my head.

If my dad wasn't really my dad and that other guy was, then . . . what if I had a twin?

I mean, if it was possible that the man who'd raised me wasn't my biological dad, then anything was really possible right now.

But I kept that theory silent. I needed to chew on the idea more.

Instead, I continued to watch as the woman on the screen smiled brightly at the camera as if she had done this a million times before. She even had my mannerisms down pat.

As she started sharing about my background, I realized that—to use one of the phrases I'd grown up with—she knew my story like the back of her hand.

She talked about growing up in a small Virginia mountain town with a single father. How she'd done some local theater. How she'd gone on to become a hairdresser before she'd been discovered.

"Anyway," Fake Joey continued. "I just want you all to know how much I love and adore all my fantastic fans. Since I'm currently not filming, I want to use this time to connect with my fans as much as possible. If you see me out in public, come talk. The more the merrier! I also have more things planned as a part of my Fan Appreciation Week. You're not going to want to miss them, so stay tuned."

"Fan Appreciation Week?" My mouth gaped open. "What in the world is this woman planning?"

"Good question."

"And 'if you see me in public, come talk'? My whole life will be totally disrupted if people do that whenever I'm out!"

"You're right." Jackson shook his head as he leaned back on the couch. "I can't believe someone would have the audacity to go this far. She could be arrested for fraud, you know. This goes beyond someone who's trying to look like their favorite celebrity."

"I've seen a lot of things in my days but never this." I glanced at the sticky note on the back of my computer. "Amanda—the reporter—gave me this woman's phone number."

"Have you tried to call her yet?"

I shook my head. "Not yet. But now that you're here, maybe you can help me make sense of this, so I don't do something irrational. Should I call her?"

Jackson straightened before offering a definitive nod. "Yeah, let's call her. Let's see what she has to say. Most likely, it will be nothing. But we should give it a shot."

I drew in a deep breath before dialing her number.

What would I say when she answered? I was going to wing it, I decided. But things never seemed to go well when I did that. Yet I couldn't seem to stop myself from trying.

Which apparently was the definition of insanity. Doing the same thing over and over again and expecting different results.

This could be a total disaster.

But at least I had Jackson beside me to act as the yin to my yang.

The phone rang four times before voicemail picked up.

"Hey, this is Joey Darling. Sorry I missed your call. Leave me a message, and I'll get back with you ASAP. And that's no *baloney*."

My bottom lip dropped open.

Baloney? It was one of my signature moves as Raven Remington, but my father had actually taught me the self-defense move in real life.

The story was that when you got into a jam, you kicked somebody below the knee. On my TV show I always yelled, "Baloney!" when I did it.

This woman was irritating me enough that my nostrils were starting to flare.

What exactly was I going to do about this?

CHAPTER
FIVE

I GLANCED at Jackson as I lowered my phone back into my lap. I hadn't left a voicemail for her. Not yet.

"What should I do now?" I asked.

"You should definitely file a police report so you have this on record. In the meantime, I'll tell my officers to keep an eye out for her."

"What about the cell phone number? Is there a chance that we could track it?"

Jackson grimaced before shaking his head. "It's a possibility. But it's most likely a burner, so we wouldn't be able to get any personal information from it. And in order to track the user's location, there are a lot of hoops we'd have to jump through first—including getting a warrant. I'm not exactly sure I'm there yet."

I let out a pent-up breath. "How else can I try to find her? I need to confront her about this before she does something really stupid. It's been a long, hard road trying to get my reputation back, and now she has a possibility of ruining it."

I'd been married to a man named Eric Lauderdale, who was also an actor and most famous for his role as Captain Gorgeous. But he'd been abusive and had actually pushed me down the stairs in our home, spit on me, and left me there to suffer. When I'd split from him, he'd done everything possible to paint me in a bad light.

That time in my life hadn't been fun, to put it lightly. I hadn't been sure I'd ever fully bounce back.

"You said this woman has been posting on social media?" Jackson narrowed his eyes as he studied my face.

I nodded. "Dizzy and her friends have been following it more than I have. But do you think maybe we could find clues in those videos?"

"I'd say it's a definite possibility."

"Let me see if I can find some of her handles on social media." No doubt it would be something like "Official Joey Darling" or something that could seem legit while not being legit at all. Maybe it would even be "The Real Joey Darling."

As I began to search social media, my thoughts

drifted to the man who'd claimed to be my father. I needed to tell Jackson about him also.

But telling him about this man now seemed like it could muddy the waters, like I'd be throwing too much on him at once.

Maybe I needed to handle this problem first, and then I could tell Jackson about my supposed dad a little later tonight.

That seemed like a good, logical plan. That's what I was trying to have in my life lately.

Logic.

I poked around a few more minutes until I found the woman's social media handles.

She *was* using "The Real Joey Darling," that little scoundrel!

Jackson and I clicked on a couple of videos. One of them showed the woman outside the grocery store today, eating up all the attention from her admirers.

My twin had also posted on the beach earlier. But nothing was in the background except the ocean. There weren't any piers or boats that would identify where exactly she was. A third video showed her at Willie Wahoos, a bar owned by a man I sometimes referred to as my nemesis.

Nothing but trouble happened at that place, and I avoided it whenever I could.

Even the bartender, Billy Corbina, seemed to think she really was me.

I scowled before focusing that negative energy.

"Does it say when this account opened?" I peered at the screen and spotted the answer. "Yes, it does. Only four days ago."

"Interesting." Jackson pointed to something at the bottom of the screen. "Look at this."

The faker was about to go live. Again.

I braced myself for whatever she might say this time.

A moment later, her face—complete with a bright smile—filled the screen selfie-style. "I have the most amazing news."

She reached beside her and pulled someone else into the camera frame with her.

My heart nearly stopped when I saw who it was.

The man who claimed to be my father was with her—though he tried to shield his face from the camera.

"Today, I got to meet my real dad for the first time," Fake Joey said. "Isn't that so incredibly exciting?"

"What?" Jackson asked with an exasperated sigh. "Who in the world is that man?"

I rubbed my hands against my pants. "That's something I actually wanted to talk to you about . . ."

Jackson now paced in front of me as he rubbed his jaw. "This man claims to be your father? I can't believe you didn't tell me."

I'd given him a brief recap of our conversation. "I was going to, but this other situation seemed more urgent, and I didn't want to throw too much on you at once."

"Thanks for that, Joey, but you don't have to protect me. I work these cases for a living, and I juggle multiple things at once. I think I could've handled this."

I shrugged. "I was trying to be considerate."

He paused and let out a breath. "You've never seen this man before today?"

"There's something about him that seems familiar, but I'm not sure if that's because we share some similar characteristics or if maybe he's been watching me or something. It's just really hard to say."

"What's this man's name?"

"I only know his first name."

"And . . . ?" Jackson twisted his head as he waited.

I didn't even want to say it. Finally, I muttered, "Adolf."

Jackson leaned closer. "Say that again."

I sighed before raising my voice just slightly. "Adolf."

"I need you to talk a little louder."

"Adolf!" I practically shouted. "He said his name was Adolf."

Jackson blanched. "That's an unfortunate name."

"Tell me about it."

He began pacing again. "Do you know where he's staying?"

"He just gave me this." I pulled the man's card from my pocket.

"He has a business card with only a phone number?" Jackson's eyes narrowed, and his lips pulled back in a grimace. "Seems like an awfully covert, CIA type of thing."

My breath caught at his words. "Do you think there's some validity to his story?"

He ran a hand through his hair. "I really have no idea."

Another thought hit me, and my hand pressed against my heart. "Jackson . . . what if my dad sees this woman's videos? What if this is how he finds out this man claims to be my father?"

"You don't think he'll realize when he sees this other Joey Darling that it's not really you?" Jackson studied me cautiously.

I knew what he was getting at, but . . . "I mean,

the camera quality isn't great, so this woman *does* look, act, and sound like me. Unless you're studying the video for validity, I could see where someone in passing would think she *was* me."

Jackson frowned and let out a moan. "This whole thing is a mess."

"This woman apparently tricked Ad . . ."

Jackson stared at me, but I wasn't sure the word would leave my lips.

"Ad . . . Adolf," I finally got out, "into thinking she was me." I shook my head before burying my face in my hands. "What in the world am I going to do?"

Just as I asked the question, glass shattered.

Jackson threw me down on the couch as the air around us became electrified.

Then another sound registered.

We were being shot at, I realized.

You *had* to be kidding me . . .

CHAPTER
SIX

"STAY DOWN!" Jackson yelled.

I ducked behind the couch, my body covering Ripley's, as more glass broke. A smoky scent filled the air.

Bullets, I realized.

That was the smell of a gun firing bullets.

Terror filled me.

I wished I could say I'd never been in a situation like this before.

But I had.

More times than I could count.

But never at my house.

My new house that I'd so lovingly purchased and decorated. The place where I was supposed to be making a home and good memories with Jackson.

"What did you do now?" Jackson muttered in

my ear.

"Me?" My mouth dropped open. "Why does it always have to be me?"

Jackson didn't say anything.

He didn't have to.

To be fair, it usually *was* me.

Jackson grabbed his phone and barked something to the person on the other line. No doubt, he was calling his colleagues at the police station to report what was happening.

As soon as he ended the call, he drew his own gun and crouched. "Stay here."

"Jackson . . ."

But it was too late to stop him.

While he left me behind the safety of the couch, he went to check out what was happening.

It was like they always said. There were people who ran away from danger and those who ran toward it. Jackson, of course, always ran toward it.

Actually, he didn't really run—he sprinted toward it like a superhero.

Unfortunately, I seemed to do the same thing, but I was much less trained and a whole lot clumsier.

An eerie silence suddenly stretched through the air.

The bullets seemed to have stopped.

But you could never be too careful.

I didn't allow myself to breathe. To relax.

Not until I knew for sure that the danger had passed.

I couldn't stop myself from peeking up to see what was happening. To see if Jackson was okay.

I spotted him pressing himself against the wall near the door. The picture window at the front of my house was shattered, just as I'd thought.

As tires squealed outside, Jackson threw the door open and ran out.

At just that moment, another round of bullets sprayed through the air.

My heart felt like it stopped.

Jackson . . .

What if he'd been shot?

I scrambled from behind the safety of my couch and darted toward the door.

When I reached it, I spotted Jackson crouching behind his truck.

He was okay.

Physically, at least.

The stormy expression on his face made it clear he wasn't very happy about this turn of events.

I waited until I was sure the shooter was gone before rushing to meet him. "Did you get a license plate?"

He stood and shoved his gun back into his

holster, still staring as the car disappeared in the distance.

"I got a partial at least." He turned toward me and studied me with his gaze. "Are you okay?"

I nodded. I was shaken but unharmed. That was really all I could ask for.

I could replace windows and furniture.

I couldn't replace lives.

"I'm fine," I assured him. "You?"

"Yeah." But the way Jackson said the word made it clear he was irritated.

And rightfully so.

Who would have done this?

As we waited for other officers to show up, Jackson was already outside looking for evidence.

Of course.

He lived for his job. He absolutely loved it, and he was good at it.

He was kind of my hero in that way.

Because, even though he loved his job, I knew he loved me more. I had no doubt about that.

I watched as he knelt on the sandy grass in front of our house and studied something.

I wanted to walk across the lawn and look also, to

see what he was doing.

But I didn't want to disturb any evidence.

Again, been there and done that before. Had the reputation to prove it, though I'd prefer some type of merit award badge. Too bad they didn't offer those for making mistakes.

He reached into his pocket and pulled out a pen. A moment later, he held up what appeared to be a shell casing.

That wasn't surprising, considering the number of bullets that had blasted us.

Jackson reached into his pocket again, this time pulling out a plastic bag—he often carried them with him—and slipped the bullet inside. He held it eye-level to study it.

When he was done, he paced back toward me. "Do you recognize this?"

I had no idea why he'd ask me something like that. Like I was some kind of expert on bullets or something . . . who did he think I was—Raven Remington?

But I hoped that didn't show on my face. Instead, I shook my head. "No, just that it's a casing."

"If I had to guess, this bullet is from a Sig Sauer 226."

"Is that supposed to mean something to me?" I really had no idea where he was going with this. I didn't even remember referencing that on *Relentless*, if that's what he was thinking.

Not that Hollywood usually got it right.

"This is from a standard issue gun that CIA operatives use," he finally explained.

It took a moment for his words to sink in. "Wait . . . what?"

Certainly, I hadn't understood him correctly.

But I knew I had.

I hadn't done anything recently to make anyone mad at me or to make myself a target. However . . .

If the man claiming to be my dad was telling the truth, then he worked for the . . . CIA.

My gaze met Jackson's. "You think this has something to do with my fake dad?"

"He's the only one who makes sense." Jackson frowned and rubbed his jaw. "His sudden presence in your life is the only reason I can think of that someone would drive by and do something like this."

"Are you sure this doesn't have anything to do with one of your cases?"

He squinted before letting his head slowly fall to the side. "Maybe. But doubtful."

I shivered at his words.

I hadn't even been looking for trouble this time.

But trouble had most definitely found me.

CHAPTER
SEVEN

AFTER THE POLICE had shown up and Jackson and I had given our statements, officers then put an APB out on the car.

I didn't have much hope they'd locate it, but you never knew.

Whoever was in the vehicle had apparently shot four other houses along the street—not just ours. That made our original theory a little murkier. Why hit so many houses if this was connected with me and Fake Dad?

Jackson had nailed some plywood over the window so no one could get into our house.

Then he'd insisted we go to his old bachelor pad to stay for the night.

Before we were married, he'd had his own cottage. We talked about either selling it or making it a rental property. But we hadn't had time to do either yet.

Therefore, we still had a place to stay tonight. With Ripley, of course.

I liked having a new place of our own. Mostly because Jackson had been married before, but his wife had died. That had been their place, and I could still feel the memories there.

I wasn't intimidated by those facts, but I wanted Jackson and me to make our own memories.

Despite that, I could stay there a few days. I mean, the decision made sense. We'd be safer there.

In theory.

Although, if someone had found me at my new house, there was a good chance they could find me wherever I went.

I shivered again.

After packing a few items, we loaded Ripley in Jackson's SUV. I hopped in my own car so I'd be free to come and go, and then we headed out.

Fifteen minutes later, we arrived at his cottage.

The place was located near Jockey's Ridge, a gigantic sand dune where people liked to hang glide, sand sled, and frolic in the sun. His cottage stood on stilts, like most of the homes in the area. His fishing boat still rested on a trailer beneath the house, and various beach items were scattered about.

The interior featured a worn leather couch, faded driftwood-hewn floors, and a stone-faced fireplace.

By the time we arrived, I was wound up. I had *way* too much on my mind to settle down.

As Jackson and I stood in his living room—I mean, *our* living room, I suppose—I pulled the business card from my pocket and stared at the ten digits there. "I think we should call Adolf."

Jackson raised his eyebrows before nodding slowly, yet briefly. "Are you sure?"

I nodded. "If this guy knows something that's going on here, I want to know."

"He and your impersonator could even be working together."

"Exactly! If I call him, do you think you can track his location? Isn't there some kind of app you could use on the down low or something? I'm pretty sure we did that once in an episode of *Relentless*."

He frowned. "It's more complicated than they show on TV."

"That doesn't answer my question."

He raised his eyebrows. "I'll see what I can do. But you need to keep him talking for at least two minutes."

"I should be able to do that." Talking was my gift. More than one person had said so.

"Okay then." Jackson nodded. "Let's do it. Put

the phone on speaker and tell him that we want to meet. I want to see this guy face-to-face."

"Of course."

My fingers trembled as I dialed the number. To my surprise, Adolf answered on the first ring.

I didn't really know where to start. I had so much I wanted to say.

So I dove right in. "You were duped. That woman you met with who claimed to be me . . . she wasn't me."

"Joey?" Surprise lilted his voice.

"Yes. Who else do you know who'd say that? Do you have any other supposed daughters you went on camera with saying you'd recently found each other?"

"It's not like that . . ."

"For someone who worked in intelligence, I'm a little surprised you weren't able to tell the difference between me and her. Aren't details supposed to be your specialty? Didn't your life depend on that?"

"I . . . I don't know what to say. After you and I met this morning at the restaurant, this woman showed up at the beach. Everything transpired from there."

My stomach tightened with irritation. "Did she tell you anything else?"

"Only that she'd be in touch later. Are you *sure* that wasn't you?"

I scowled, though Adolf couldn't see me. "I'm positive."

"It just doesn't make sense . . ."

"Look, I'd really like to meet. My husband would like to come also."

"When?"

"Tonight?"

A barely perceptible sigh passed. "I can't. I'm sorry. I have something else going on."

Something else? I thought he'd come into town to talk to me.

So what else could he have scheduled? Watching a game on TV? Searching for ghost crabs on the beach?

I supposed it didn't matter, but I had something else I needed to say to him before this conversation ended. "Is there any reason someone who knows you might have come to my house and tried to kill me tonight?"

"Excuse me?" Surprise climbed through his voice.

"As I was sitting in my living room talking to my husband, someone drove past and sprayed about twenty bullets into my house."

He gasped, sounding truly shocked. "Are you okay?"

"Thankfully, I'm fine. But I want to know if you had anything to do with it."

"Of course I didn't have anything to do with it. Why would you even ask that?" A wounded tone stained his voice.

"Because you're the only reason I can think of that someone might have come after me."

He paused. "Joey . . . I don't know what to say. I wish I could talk more. I really do. But I need to go."

Before I could ask any more questions, the phone line went dead.

I glanced at Jackson on the couch beside me. "Well? Did you track him?"

He frowned and shook his head. "You didn't make it two minutes."

My mouth dropped open. "What? Are you sure?"

"Positive."

I sighed. "Some things *are* just like the movies. Case in point."

"Joey . . . I was kidding about the two-minute thing. It doesn't really work like that in real life."

I gave him a dirty look. "Very funny."

He shrugged playfully before continuing to look

at his laptop. "Let's see what I can find out on this guy here."

I leaned closer to Jackson, laying my head on his shoulder as I stared at the computer.

I gave him several minutes before I asked, "Anything?"

He let out a long breath. "Apparently, there are many men with the name Adolf."

"Really?" My pitch climbed with surprise.

"Yes, really. We don't even know if that's his real name. But, to answer your question, no. I haven't found anything. I knew it was a longshot."

"If we were to ask, he'd probably say he was using an alias because he was CIA." I snorted at the ridiculous thought.

This whole thing was mind-boggling.

I sat up straight and stretched my legs out on the coffee table in front of me. "Let's see. I don't know who Fake Dad really is. I don't know who Fake Joey is. I don't know where either of these people are staying or if they're even in this together. Nor do I know what they—either collectively or individually —are planning next. That's a lot of unknowns."

Jackson gave my knee a gentle squeeze. "We'll keep looking for more information. Hopefully, my guys will run across either the fake Joey, your fake dad, or the driver of that car that drove past and shot at the house."

"Those seem like some pretty lofty hopes." I frowned.

"Part of it is hope. Part of it is skill. Another part is training and perseverance. We'll get this."

I locked my gaze with his. "I love it when you sound so professional."

His eyes warmed. "Do you?"

"I most definitely do." Then I reached up and planted a long kiss on his lips, forever grateful Jackson was in my life.

THE NEXT MORNING, Jackson left for work—but not before warning me to be careful and remain alert.

I'd already arranged for my best friend, Phoebe, to come over.

Just as I finished making some yogurt parfaits, a knock sounded at the door.

Phoebe was right on time.

Phoebe was the sister of Jackson's deceased wife, which might sound weird, but it wasn't.

My friend was a down-to-earth petite blonde who avoided makeup and hair products, yet still looked amazing and naturally beautiful. She loved the beach and had a laid-back attitude I'd love to emulate.

That attitude made her easy to get along with but hard to read.

She worked at a smoothie shop called Oh Buoy and also ran a dog-sitting and dog-walking business.

Not terribly long ago, she'd begun dating my *Relentless* costar, Sam Butler. The two were doing the long-distance thing, but they seemed happy. Sam was supposed to come into town next week to visit her, and I knew Phoebe was looking forward to it.

We sat down in the kitchen with some coffee and yogurt, and I gave her the rundown on everything that happened.

"Wait . . ." She shifted and pulled a leg beneath her on the wooden chair. "Do you think the timing of this is coincidental?"

"For all I know, those two are working together." I paused a moment before blurting my next theory. "What if I have a twin?"

I was going to keep that brainstorm quiet, but I changed my mind.

"A twin?"

I grabbed my computer and pulled up a video of my look-alike. Then I played it for Phoebe.

"I mean, it's eerie how much she looks, sounds, and acts like me." Even watching it a second time I thought so.

"You're right." Phoebe squinted as she studied the images. "It is eerie. But a twin . . . ?"

"I know it sounds crazy. I can't even believe I'm

voicing the theory out loud because it sounds more like something that happens in a Lifetime movie. But if I just let go of my own emotions and brainstorm—and there are no bad ideas when you brainstorm—then what if this guy really *is* my dad? That would mean that there's a whole bunch about my life that I don't know. Maybe my mom had twins and gave the other one away."

"But your mom and dad were married when you were born. That means that your dad—your real dad—would have known that twins were born. I don't think he would have let siblings be separated like that."

I frowned as I slowly acknowledged the truth in her statement. She was right. My dad wouldn't have let that happen.

So . . . scratch that theory.

But I just didn't understand this.

"Maybe this woman had plastic surgery, and she's a really good actress, and *that's* how she's able to imitate your voice and mannerisms," Phoebe suggested as she crossed her arms, like a lawyer making her closing statement.

"I suppose that's a possibility." And it was.

But there was so much I didn't know.

I let out a sigh and then hit the newest video, the one that had been blasted over social media last night. The one where Fake Joey claimed to have discovered her real father.

I played it for Phoebe to give her a better feel of what was going on here.

Her hand covered her mouth as she watched. "That's just unnerving, Joey."

"I know! Whoever this woman is, she's in this 100 percent."

"More like psycho percent . . . okay, that didn't make sense. But you know what I'm saying."

I did. There was dedication . . . and then there was unsettling obsession.

I frowned as I stared at the screen. "I'm afraid Dad will see it, and I'm not even sure what he's going to think. What if he thinks that Joey really is me?"

Phoebe offered a compassionate frown. "I think a father always knows, right? He'll know it's not you."

"I hope that's true."

"Wait . . ." Phoebe sat up straighter. "Pause it right there."

I did as she said.

"Now back up like three seconds."

Again, I did as she said.

Then she pointed at the upper left-hand corner of the screen.

I could barely see it, but some type of purple dragon kite flew on the beach.

"That's a pretty unique kite." Phoebe's voice climbed with excitement—at least, this was as close as she ever got to excitement, which was still pretty low-key.

"It is, but how is that going to help me? It's not as if that's a permanent fixture here on the island."

"I know, but usually when people fly fancy kites like this, they're in town for about a week, and they go to the same places to fly the kites—whatever beach is closest to their rental."

I sucked in a breath.

My friend was brilliant.

I sat up straighter, excitement racing through me. "So if I can find whoever's flying the kite, I can narrow down the section of the beach where my fake dad might be staying . . ."

Phoebe shrugged. "That's my theory."

I threw my arms around her. "You're amazing. Thank you."

She let out a little chuckle. "No problem."

Now I just needed to figure out when the best time was to go to the beach and search for that kite.

Phoebe stayed another couple of hours, and we caught up with each other.

Then at lunchtime, Jackson came home bearing chicken and veggie bowls from a new restaurant in town. He looked tired, like whatever case he was working bogged him down.

He hadn't told me about his latest investigation, and I figured it was better that way. Especially since I tended to insert myself in whatever mysteries came my way.

Who would've known that would be such a fun hobby for me?

Although hobby was probably an understatement.

He pressed a quick kiss on my lips before saying, "I have about two hours for lunch and so I thought I'd come home and check on you."

I took the bag from him. "Perfect. Because I have a plan of what we need to do."

"Oh, do you?" He raised his eyebrows.

"Yes, I do. I have a video to show you." I unloaded the food on the table so we could eat while we talked.

"A video?" He frowned as he sat down. "Is it the fake Joey again?"

"Yes. I mean, no. Well . . . yes and no."

He tilted his head. "That sounds a little weird . . ."

"I know. It is a bit odd, but wait until you see . . ."

As we sat at the table, I showed him the footage of the kite flying behind Fake Dad and Fake Joey.

"A kite's in the background? Okay . . ." He let out a breath before nodding. "I suppose this is a good lead to check out. Besides, it's a beautiful day outside, so what can it hurt, right?"

"Exactly. Let's eat and then go."

We quickly ate our lunch and then grabbed Ripley. As soon as we climbed into Jackson's work SUV, my phone rang.

It was Amanda Walters.

"Hi, Amanda." I put the phone on speaker so Jackson could hear.

"Joey . . ." She sounded trepid as she said my name. "I've been having lots of long talks here with my producer. Things have gotten a little ugly. He's not very happy I was duped, and I can't blame him. We want to be a trustworthy news source, and this one almost got over on us. The fact that we were advertising the interview is only making things worse."

"I'm sorry to hear that." I rubbed Ripley's head as he poked his nose between Jackson and me from the back.

"It was supposed to air tonight as our feature story."

"All right . . ." I wasn't sure where she was going with this.

"Instead, I was wondering . . ." Her voice trailed with uncertainty.

"Yes?"

"I was wondering if . . . okay, I'm just going to come right out and ask. I was wondering if you might want to do a story talking about how this woman is impersonating you." The rest of her words came out rushed with apprehension.

My spine tightened at that thought. *"Really?"*

I glanced at Jackson, trying to get his reaction.

His eyes narrowed as if he wasn't sure what he thought about that idea.

"I know this is a lot to consider," Amanda continued.

I peered out the window at the various gift shops we passed on the main drag. Some could be found at any beach along the East Coast. Others were local and folksy.

I wished I was shopping at one of them instead of having this conversation.

"I'm going to need to think about it," I finally told her.

Jackson nodded as if he approved of that answer.

"Listen, I know this isn't your problem," Amanda said. "And I know reporters haven't exactly been your best friends in the past. But if there's any way you could give me an answer by this afternoon, that would be great. That way, if you're interested, we could set up the interview maybe for tomorrow so we can begin advertising this new story. It would go a long way with my boss."

I wanted to say she was right: this wasn't my problem. Because it *wasn't* my problem.

But, just as before, I kind of felt bad for the woman.

"I'll give you a call back today," I finally murmured. "I promise."

"Thank you so much."

I ended the call and glanced at Jackson. "What do you think?"

His jaw tightened. "I can see advantages and disadvantages of going public with this. The disadvantage is that you're putting all your business out there for people to know and people tend to exploit things like that."

"Yet I'm already being exploited, so how much worse can it get?"

He waved a finger in the air. "Never ask that."

I bit down. "You're right. I shouldn't ask that. And the advantage?"

"The advantage would be that you're taking control of the situation," Jackson said. "Instead of letting these people call all the shots, you're calling them."

"I like that."

"Plus, we don't know what else this woman has planned. What if she tries to con people somehow? To ask people for money? If she tells men she's Joey Darling in order to take advantage of them?"

"I thought only men did stuff like that . . ." Maybe that wasn't the thought he wanted to leave me with, but . . . *did* women do stuff like that?

"You might be surprised."

I sucked in a deep breath before letting out a long sigh. "Sounds like I have a lot to think about."

"You do." We pulled to a stop at one of the public beach accesses. "But for now, let's take a walk and look for that kite."

CHAPTER
NINE

JACKSON PARKED NEAR THE BEACH. I quickly pulled on my baseball cap and sunglasses— yes, I kept some in his SUV also—and we walked toward the oceanfront with Ripley happily trotting in front of us, his tongue hanging from his mouth and tail raised.

That dog loved the beach.

The weather today was in the low eighties and felt perfect. This wasn't the busiest part of the summer season, so the sandy shores weren't as crowded as they would be in the coming weeks.

Truthfully, the beaches in the Outer Banks were never super crowded, not compared to the other resort beaches. Vacationers lounging on the shore usually had a good ten feet between their setup and other people's—and that was on a busy day.

I continued toward the ocean. Getting some exercise felt good. But it really felt good to spend more time with Jackson.

As we walked with Ripley on the uneven sand near the crashing waves, the scent of the ocean rose around us—salty with hints of seaweed. Mixed with that was the smell of hot sand and the aroma of coconut-scented sunscreen.

The combination was pretty much one of my favorites in the whole world.

I mulled over Amanda's request with every step.

"What do you think I should do?" I asked Jackson, careful to step over a washed-up jellyfish. "Any more thoughts on my conversation with that reporter?"

With his hands in his pockets, he stared straight ahead, clearly thinking it over. If there was one thing I could always count on from Jackson, it was that he was thoughtful and purposeful with his words. I admired—and sometimes envied—that about him.

"I don't know, Joey." His jaw tightened as he frowned. "Do you really want to put all of your dirty laundry out there?"

"But if I don't, what if the media spins this situation into something it isn't?"

His twisted his head, lips pressed together. "I guess I've never been in your position before. But I know you've mentioned wanting your privacy. I'd hate to see you put this out there only to have it exploited."

"I don't want that." Just the word "exploited" made me feel so exposed. Eric—my ex—had preyed on my vulnerabilities every chance he got, which made me even more sensitive to these things. People who preyed on other's weaknesses were the lowest of the low.

"I mean, how much attention do you want from this?" Jackson continued. "Because it could implode on you. You could get calls from magazines and TV stations wanting interviews. A situation like this has the potential to go national. Is that something you're willing to face?"

I frowned at his question and tugged my hat lower as the sun bore down on us. The truth was, I didn't know. "Having a mischievous and possibly devious impersonator isn't really what I want to be known for, if that's what you're asking."

"It sounds like something you may need to think over then."

He was right. In the least, I needed to sleep on it.

But I'd told Amanda I'd give her an answer today. That answer would most likely be, "I still don't know."

"You also need to consider what else this woman

might have up her sleeves," Jackson continued. "Right now, her antics all seem to be about getting attention. But she could take this to another level—one that harms your reputation."

I frowned again. He was absolutely right. If people really thought Fake Joey was me, then her actions would reflect on me. There were people out there who wouldn't believe she was my doppelganger.

As Jackson, Ripley, and I continued down the shore, I scanned everything around me.

Families played on the beach, surfers surfed, fishermen set up their gear on the shoreline.

But no kite.

I knew finding it would be a long shot. Even if the person with that kite was staying nearby, there was no guarantee they'd be out right now.

But at least I was doing *something* to find answers. It beat staying cooped up inside all day. Sure, I'd been sent scripts to read. I probably needed to talk to my manager and tell him what was going on. I'd also promised to do a ribbon-cutting ceremony at a local museum this week, and I needed to read all the emails about that.

But . . . I had other things on my mind.

I let out a breath and decided to change the subject. "So . . . it seems like whatever case you're working on right now has you really bogged down."

I knew Jackson didn't like to talk about these things. But I'd seen the stress in his eyes when he got home from work on most days—provided he did get home from work. I mean, sure, he came home to sleep. But sometimes he put in eighteen-hour days.

I'd known about the reality of his schedule before we got married, and I was okay with it. As long as he stayed healthy, that was. Sometimes in jobs like Jackson's, it was easy to lose yourself in other people's problems. I didn't want that to happen.

In my own way, keeping my eye on him was how *I* could protect *him* for a change—by monitoring his mental health.

"It's a long story." He moved closer to me as an obnoxious wave tried to tag him.

I knew by his tone that he didn't want to talk about it, which disappointed me more than it should.

Of course, I wished we could both share every aspect of our lives. But because of Jackson's job there were limitations. I could respect that.

Which meant I wasn't sure why I asked, "Could you just give me a hint?"

"Does not knowing bother you?" Jackson stole a glance at me.

I rubbed my lips together as I contemplated how

to answer. I supposed honesty was the best policy, right? That's what everyone always said.

But I also didn't want Jackson to think I was being nosy.

Because I *was* nosy.

"Well, the truth is—" I started.

Before I could finish, Jackson pointed to something in the distance.

I looked up in the sky, and my mouth dropped open.

I couldn't believe it.

A big purple dragon kite launched into the air directly in front of us.

Forty feet down the beach, I spotted a ten- or eleven-year-old boy holding onto a kite-string reel. His mom sunbathed in a chair nearby, sunglasses covering her eyes. The dad played in the water, trying to catch a wave. At least, I assumed those were his parents since they were the closest adults.

I decided to carefully approach the boy, knowing it wasn't exactly smiled upon when a stranger talked to kids.

"Excuse me." I paused a safe distance away. "Is

your mom or dad around here? I have a question about your kite."

The sunbathing woman sat up right then, a suspicious look in her gaze. "Can I help you?"

Her eyes widened when she saw me. She was trying to place me, wasn't she?

It happened a lot.

"I'm sorry to intrude," I started. "But were you flying this kite on the beach late yesterday?"

"Yes, we were out here flying it." The woman pushed her white, thick plastic sunglasses back up on her tiny nose. "Why do you ask?"

"Somebody was taking a video right in this area around the same time. I was wondering if you might have seen them."

"Oh, that's right." She snapped her fingers. "I did see them. I remember thinking the woman looked like . . ." She pulled her sunglasses down again. "Joey Darling. Wait . . . was that *you*?"

I shook my head. "It wasn't me out here."

"Well, the woman could've been a dead ringer for you. Honestly, I felt a little starstruck." She puckered her lips as she stared at me. "I mean, I didn't recognize you at first, not with that baseball hat and oversized sunglasses. But really . . . the similarities are uncanny."

"I understand." I tugged at my hat, which proclaimed, "I'll Bring the Shenanigans."

The Hot Chicks had given it to me. Dizzy had one that said, "I'll Bring the Trouble." MaryAnn's said, "I'll Bring the Good Vibes." Maxine's said, "I'll Bring the Alibi" and Geraldine's, "I'll Bring the Food."

The woman turned away from me and waved her hand at the man in the water. "Hey, honey! Come over here. You'll never believe this. It's Joey Darling!"

At once, people seemed to appear out of nowhere —not just this woman's husband.

Anyone who'd heard her crept closer, forming a circle around me.

My blood pressure climbed. This was not what I needed right now.

Jackson pushed the crowd back to give me some space.

"I'm actually trying to find this person," I explained to her as I lowered my voice. "I was just wondering if you saw which direction the people filming that video may have gone when they left?"

"Oh, yes. It was hard to miss. When they left this area, the woman climbed into a red sports car parked just over the dune."

A red sports car? Give me a break. Fake Joey really was working hard to imitate me.

"And the man?" I asked.

The woman shrugged. "He went in the opposite direction. I'm not sure where, to be honest."

"Was there anything else that stood out?" Jackson moved closer.

The woman chewed on her bottom lip. "Not that I can think of. She and the man she was with seemed as if they were having a good time together."

My back muscles tightened.

Having a good time together?

What were the chances that Fake Joey and Fake Dad knew each other before all of this? Was I being punked?

So many questions raced through my head.

"Thanks for your time." Jackson nodded at the woman.

He put his hand on my back and began leading me away.

I hadn't learned much useful information on this little walk, but at least I now had a basic location where Fake Joey might be staying and a description of her car.

Something was better than nothing.

CHAPTER
TEN

TWENTY MINUTES LATER, Jackson had stationed an officer near the walkover leading to that area of the beach. Officer Walburg would keep an eye open for my look-alike and/or the man claiming to be my father.

Jackson also put an APB out for the red sports car. Although there was one main road splitting the island, there were a lot of backroads and enough tourists coming and going that I knew locating the car would be like finding a needle in a haystack.

Jackson had to go back to work, so we climbed into his white official police SUV and started to his place.

As he pulled onto the street, he muttered something beneath his breath before pressing on the accelerator.

I took a gulp of air. "What are you doing?"

I was missing something.

"I just saw the car that the shooter was driving last night." He craned his neck to see through traffic.

My heart pounded faster. "Are you sure?"

"One hundred percent." Jackson clenched his jaw as he did a U-turn.

He was in a full-on police mode right now—and I liked it. I liked it *a lot*.

He turned on his lights and siren and headed down the busy road. Then he called the station so other officers could also be on the lookout.

But traffic blocked us. One vehicle would get out of his way, only for someone else to dart in front of him.

People really had no clue what to do when they heard sirens, did they? Especially if the roads were crowded.

"Come on," Jackson muttered before pressing on his horn.

The car in front of us finally pulled to the side of the road, allowing Jackson through.

As I glanced ahead of us, I didn't see the car anywhere.

It couldn't have just disappeared into thin air . . . right?

We'd been so close . . . but it appeared we'd lost them.

Jackson checked out our cottage before giving me a kiss on the cheek and then returning to work. His departing words were a warning to be careful.

Of course.

I was *always* careful.

Until I wasn't.

After watching him leave, I stepped back inside the cottage and locked the door before crossing my arms. I turned toward the living room and sighed as I leaned back against the door.

I still wasn't sure if Fake Dad and Fake Joey were out to harm me or just get something from me.

That gunfire last night? Was it directed at me? Or did I just happen to be a random house on a street where the shots occurred? There were other shots fired at other houses on the street.

I just didn't know what to think.

I only stayed inside the house for five minutes before restlessness got the best of me.

I looked at Ripley, who sat staring up at me and wagging his tail as if he knew I had something on my mind.

Because I did.

There was someone—a few someones, actually—who just might have some answers for me.

But I'd need to pay these people a visit in person, and if I didn't show up within the next fifteen minutes, I'd be too late.

"I need to make a quick stop," I told Ripley. "Can you stay here for a little while by yourself?"

He barked.

I put my hand to my ear. "What was that? Do you want me to get out of the house for a while so you can have some alone time with that ham bone I promised you?"

He barked again.

"It's a deal." I rubbed his head and ears, swishing them back and forth affectionately before grabbing the ham bone for him.

I jumped in my car and took off down the road. As I drove, I was on edge, keeping my eyes wide open for anyone suspicious.

Thankfully, I had no problems.

A few minutes later, I pulled up to the burger joint Meatsa Eatsa and rushed inside. The scent of sizzling ground beef and onions hit me, making my stomach grumble. The place ground their own beef every day, fermented their own pickles, mixed their own dressings, and pretty much bottled sunshine for any foodies traveling through the area.

I'd forgotten about how good everything smelled in here, and how it tasted even better.

Before the hostess approached me, I glanced around the space and spotted exactly who I was looking for. I gave the hostess a wave and pointed toward the table in the corner before hurrying through the restaurant.

Almost as if well-orchestrated choreography, in one graceful move I grabbed a spare chair at a nearby table and pulled it up beside the six men in the corner booth. They were eating late lunches, playing cards, and misbehaving.

"If it isn't Joey Darling." Ivan Sanderson looked up from the end of the booth, his shaggy white eyebrows raised so high it almost appeared he had hair on the top of his head again.

I glanced around the table at each of the men. Fearless leader Ivan. Hard-of-hearing Chuck. Inappropriate joke maker Lloyd. Quiet but sweet Frank. Cackling laugh Sammy. And . . . a new guy.

He must be the one the Hot Chicks were drooling over. I could see why. He had thick white hair, a sturdy build, relatively small potbelly, and minimal wrinkles.

"If it isn't the ROMEOs . . ." I loved these guys,

and so did my dad. He used to hang out with them every week. The group got together to eat, to talk, to play cards—basically, to do life together.

At the thought, my heart panged with grief.

What I wouldn't do to be able to talk to Dad again. He hadn't even been able to walk me down the aisle when I got married two months ago.

However, if my dad came out of hiding, he'd be a dead man.

For that reason, I knew I had to continue on with life and make the best of things despite how much I missed him.

"So, what brings you by?" Ivan stared at me, ignoring the onion rings that grew cold in front of him. "Unfortunately for us, you're not retired, old, or a man. Half the time, I'm not sure you eat either." He leaned closer and lowered his voice. "*Are* you eating?"

"Of course I'm eating." Why did people always ask me that?

"So . . ." Ivan continued.

I licked my lips and reminded myself that I should always check the water depth before deciding to dive in.

Then I dove in anyway.

I INHALED BEFORE JUMPING IN. "I have a question, and I know it's going to sound strange."

"Whatever you need to ask, spit it out." Lloyd, with his hawklike nose, crossed his arms and leaned back as if waiting to hear a good story.

"Is she doing laundry? She needs to spin something?" Chuck looked confused.

"I said spit it out," Lloyd corrected. "No spinning involved."

Sammy began cackling—as to be expected. Half the other guys moaned while the rest mumbled to themselves.

I rubbed my palms on my shorts, hoping I didn't regret this. The question was risky, especially since I needed to keep things under wraps. But finding answers was necessary.

"Did my dad ever happen to mention . . . ?" I hesitated, knowing how this would sound. But I needed to ask anyway. "Did he ever mention that . . . that maybe he wasn't really my father?"

Silence stretched for all of three seconds.

Then a ruckus broke out.

Yes, a ruckus.

When the men finally quieted, Cackling Sammy—with no hint of amusement in his voice—asked, "Why in the world would you ever think that, child?"

"Now, don't get your feathers ruffled, everyone." I met the gaze of each man in the circle. "It's just that someone approached me and said that he was really my dad."

Another ruckus broke out. In fact, it was such a ruckus that everyone in the restaurant seemed to turn and look at us.

This time, there was anger instead of confusion in the men's tones, however.

I hushed the men before they got even more out of control.

I needed to keep this quiet!

I leaned closer and lowered my voice. "I'm not saying it's true. But I clearly can't ask my dad."

My words seemed to sober them.

"We sure do miss him." Frank frowned and stared at his half-eaten burger.

"He was a good man," Lloyd added.

"He still *is* a good man. I never could beat him when we played chickenfoot," Sammy said. "But I sure did try."

My heart filled with both an ache and warmth.

There was so much I missed about seeing my father also. I missed his advice. His unconditional love. His stupid dad jokes.

For the longest time, I'd held onto the hope that one day, I might experience those things again.

But what if that was never possible?

"This man just wants money from you." Sammy leaned closer and jabbed his finger in the air. "Isn't that what everybody wants nowadays? A way to get rich quick."

"I think he wants fame." Lloyd glanced around the table, looking for nods of affirmation. "Everybody wants their five minutes of fame. It's this new genera-tion . . . they can't be content with a simple life."

"You said this guy wants a new flame?" Chuck cupped his hand around his ear.

"Fame, you old man!" Ivan heckled. "Maybe you should adjust your hearing aids before we all lose our minds."

"I don't have any aids, but I've thought about getting one who might come to my condo to help cook and do some light housework. Maybe someone cute . . ."

Wow, this man really *couldn't* hear well.

"Maybe he's a psycho who wants to get into your head," Frank said.

"Maybe he wants to get into more than her head!" Lloyd's eyes widened mischievously.

Sammy began to cackle again.

"Lloyd!" Frank scolded.

"I mean, maybe he wants to get into her bank account." A new innocence filled Lloyd's voice. "Get your mind out of the gutter!"

I suppressed a smile as I let the men argue.

Then I shifted in the hard wooden chair, ready to get back to business. "So my dad never mentioned anything like this to you?"

I glanced around the table, staring at each of their faces as I searched for the truth.

They each shook their heads and looked as if they'd rush to defend me if this guy ever showed up in my life again.

All except for two men—the new guy, who had no idea what was going on—and . . .

Frank Gray.

Frank *did* shake his head, but he also broke eye contact with me.

Did he know something? Frank, out of all these men, had probably been the closest with my dad. They used to go out fishing together, and they were in the same Bible study.

I needed to talk to him. One on one.

But that wouldn't be happening here. I'd need to figure out a way to make that happen later.

However, I knew his daughter had opened an ice cream store named Sprinkles in the neighboring town of Kitty Hawk. Sometimes, even though Frank was officially retired from the post office, he helped her out there.

Maybe I would pay him a visit there sometime soon.

As I left the restaurant, I ran into MaryAnn and her son, Danny. The large, gangly man had limbs he still hadn't quite grown into. But when he wore his police uniform, it somehow made him seem distinguished and less goofy.

"I wasn't expecting to see you here." I smiled at both of them despite the glaring sun overhead.

"Danny said he had some time today, so we're having lunch together." MaryAnn looped her arm through his. "Isn't that sweet that he wants to have lunch with his mom?"

The dark-haired police officer shifted and smiled almost shyly.

He was a lot like his mom in that way.

As my gaze fell on him again, an invisible brick seemed to drop on my head.

Way back before I'd known the names of most of the officers on the force, I'd given many of them nicknames.

And Danny had always been Officer Loose Lips.

The name was self-explanatory.

The man couldn't keep his mouth shut.

Under the guise of getting out of the sun, I backed away from the front door and stood in the nearby shade instead.

"I'm actually glad I ran into you," I started.

I shouldn't do this.

But I was going to.

"What's going on?" MaryAnn had that motherly tone to her voice.

"So . . . Jackson has been talking to me about the big thing that's going on at the station." I glanced at Danny, wondering if he would take the bait.

He did. "You mean, the hit that was put out?"

I used my acting skills and hid any surprise I felt, even though shock exploded inside me. "Yes, that one. How's it going? I've been worried about Jackson lately. He seems so preoccupied with it."

"We all are, and we still don't have any answers."

I licked my lips, choosing my next question carefully. "You don't know who this hit is out on?"

"No idea. But we just know that someone is willing to pay a lot of money to kill this person. Scary stuff, really."

I placed my hand over my heart. "That is just so horrible."

"I know. We're all on edge, especially after that shooting at your place last night."

"I know," I said. "I couldn't believe it. Do you think that's connected?"

He shrugged. "That's what we're trying to figure out. We're hoping to get Bronxy—that's the career criminal we arrested—to cooperate."

"Okay." MaryAnn took her son's arm and led him closer to the door. "Enough talking. Danny's entire lunch break is going to be over, and we haven't even sat down yet."

"Sorry to hold you up." I gave them both a bright smile and waved as they slipped inside the restaurant.

I felt a teensy bit guilty, but now I had a lot to think about.

An unknown person in this area had a high value hit out on them.

How interesting.

CHAPTER
TWELVE

EVEN THOUGH IT was most likely a waste of time, I'd decided to drive through town and look for any red sports cars.

Talk about a lesson in futility.

But I crisscrossed from Croatan Highway to Beach Road and then back again, trying to travel each of the side streets in an effort to be thorough.

The process would take me a long time, and that would only cover half of the island. The other half consisted of homes located on the sound side.

Plus, there was always a possibility that Fake Joey wasn't even staying on this part of the island. She could be farther north near Duck or Corolla. Or she could be farther south, in Rodanthe or on Hatteras Island. For all I knew, she could be to the west on Roanoke Island.

There were so many possibilities.

So I didn't really know why I was doing this.

I suppose it was because it was *something*, which was better than *nothing*.

That phrase kept going through my mind, probably because it was true.

But as I drove, I chewed on what I had learned so far. Most especially I chewed on what Danny had said.

I still felt a little guilty about the method I'd used to get that information.

But at least I had a little more insight now as to what was going on and why Jackson was so on edge.

Did I need to fess up to him later?

I hadn't decided that yet.

After an hour of zigzagging the streets, fighting both traffic and beachgoers, I decided I'd had enough. This was getting me nowhere.

Impulsively, I stopped in the parking lot closest to where the dragon kite had been flown earlier.

Luckily, I found a space.

I wanted to check out this beach one more time. It wasn't that I expected to see Fake Joey or even Fake Dad.

But my curiosity drove me.

As I started over the walkover, I spotted a familiar face in the distance and froze.

I released my breath, realizing I'd overreacted. It was just my friend Zane Oakley.

He paused in front of me, wetsuit clinging to his body and surfboard balanced on his head.

He was always fun. Man, the two of us could have a good time together.

But we'd also had a bit of a fling before Jackson and I got together, and I knew that Zane and me hanging out alone wasn't a realistic possibility anymore. In groups? No problem.

But I'd had to set some boundaries. Jackson and I had a long talk about it.

However, as Zane made his way toward me, I could only grin. I missed drinking smoothies together and watching Bob Ross as we made stupid jokes. Plus, he was always up for anything. If I'd needed a partner in crime, he was there.

"Long time no see," I started.

"Joey-Woey!" He used the silly nickname he'd given me.

We fist-bumped followed by a mid-air hand explosion, and then breakdancing fingers. We had our greeting worked out all the way down to the names we'd given each movement.

"I've missed you, girl," Zane muttered.

"I know, we all need to get together sometime soon." He'd just started dating a woman named Sunshine. Zane could always find someone to date—that had never been a problem for him.

I'd met Sunshine once. She was also a surfer, who made soy candles on the side and who always smelled like essential oils. She seemed nice enough, and Zane seemed pretty happy.

"Let's get it on our calendars," Zane said. "Hashtag: right now."

"Hashtag: absolutely."

We began to walk down the beach together, Zane still balancing that surfboard on top of his head.

"Weren't you leaving?" I asked.

"I was, but I'll walk with you for a while instead. So, what brings you out here? You're not wearing a bathing suit, so I assume you're not sunbathing."

"It's a long story." I pressed my lips together, blocking the words from leaving my mouth.

If I started talking about the situation now with Zane, we'd be here for a while. Then he might suggest investigating together. And that . . . well, it could cause all kinds of troubles. Not trouble because I had feelings for him. I didn't. But trouble because I was now married, and I had to be careful about who I was seen alone with.

If the paparazzi decided they wanted to paint me

in a negative light, I didn't want to give them fodder. Being alone with an old flame? I'd practically be setting myself up for trouble.

Instead, we talked about the real estate market, the new place he'd moved into, and Sunshine.

As we walked, I glanced at the sky as if expecting to see that kite there again.

It wasn't.

I scanned everyone around me, but I didn't see Fake Joey or Fake Dad either. I suppose part of me felt disappointed, even though I hadn't really expected to find them out here.

"Uh oh," Zane muttered.

I looked over and spotted two cops headed my way.

Did they have an update for me? Had Jackson sent them? Had something happened?

My spine tightened.

I pushed my nerves down and plastered on a bright smile as they approached. "Officers . . . how's everything going today?"

Neither of them smiled back.

Instead, Officer Always Serious Byron took my arms and pulled out handcuffs. The metal clasped my wrists until I lost the freedom to move my arms.

"You do know it's illegal to impersonate somebody else," he said as he led me back toward the walkover.

Wait . . . what? These officers thought I was Fake Joey! I'd even had these guys over for dinner before. How could they?

"No, you've got this all wrong," I tried to explain.

"Detective Sullivan told us that you'd probably say that."

"But I'm Jackson's wife—his real wife!" I glanced over my shoulder saying, "Tell them, Zane."

"She really is Joey!" Zane called. "Do you want me to get you a lawyer?"

I let out a sigh and shook my head.

But when I glanced around, I realized everyone around me was recording my arrest.

Social media would be the death of my career. I was certain of it.

CHAPTER
THIRTEEN

JACKSON STOOD across from me at the interrogation table at the police station.

Not that I'd officially been arrested.

In fact, the two officers who'd brought me in had received a proper scolding from Jackson about their mistake.

I knew I was free to go home, but Jackson wanted a moment with me.

I dreaded this conversation.

"Why did you go back to the beach?" Jackson asked.

"I was just curious," I explained with an innocent shrug as I lounged in one of the chairs.

"I asked you to be careful." He gave me that stare-down again before he started to pace.

"I *was* being careful. I was taking a stroll in broad daylight surrounded by other people."

"And Zane," he added.

Was that a touch of jealousy in his voice? I couldn't be sure.

Jackson wasn't usually the envious type, but animosity existed between him and Zane. It went way back to before I was even in the picture. What it boiled down to was the fact that Jackson had never fully trusted Zane. Knowing what I did about the situation, I didn't really blame him.

I took off my hat and ran a hand through my hair. "I just happened to run into Zane. I didn't arrange to meet him at the beach if that's what you're implying. Besides, even if that was the case, you know you can trust me."

"I know I can trust you. It's Zane I don't always trust." Jackson paused and gave me a pointed look.

"He respects my boundaries. He knows we're married now, and things can't be like they used to be."

Jackson leveled his gaze with me. "He still has a thing for you."

"Jackson . . ." I dropped my head to the side and gave him a stare.

He walked to the other side of the table, tugged me to my feet, then folded me in his arms. "Of course, you can hang out with whoever you want to. And, of course, I trust you. But we talked about Zane. Considering the history between the two of you . . ."

Yes, I remembered those conversations very well. I'd asked him not to use police speak around me all the time and to never, ever cut his toenails in my presence, and he'd asked me to limit my time with Zane. "I understand. It's like I said, I didn't plan on running into him. And you have nothing to worry about. You're the one I love."

"I do trust you." He cupped my face with his hands. "I just don't want to see anything happen to you."

Then he planted a tender kiss on my lips.

In the middle of it, my phone buzzed.

Dizzy had texted.

> Fake Joey just posted a new video. You'll want to see!

I held my breath as I anticipated what Fake Joey might have posted.

The video was live, so I couldn't go back to watch what she'd already said. Not yet. The live recording had to finish first.

So Jackson and I started midway through. He'd

pulled up a chair beside mine in the interrogation room, and we leaned close to watch.

My doppelganger held out her camera in selfie pose again. A cedar-planked wall stretched behind her this time, nothing on it.

Was she being careful not to leave any clues about where she was located?

Possibly.

Jackson leaned closer, his gaze intense as he watched.

"I just want to let all of my fans know just how much I love you." Her voice caught with sincerity. "You mean the absolute world to me, and I wouldn't be where I am today without you."

She paused and swallowed hard as if feigning emotion.

"As some of you might know, my home was vandalized last night. It's no longer safe for me to stay there, so I've had to move to a new location."

"How did she know about that?" Jackson muttered.

That was an excellent question.

"But as a way of thanking you all for your support, guess what?" Her eyes lit. "I'm having a party!"

My lungs froze.

I didn't like where this was going. It reminded me

of the anticipation I felt before watching myself onscreen for the first time. I felt sick to my stomach.

"So I'm inviting you all . . ." She paused dramatically. "To head over to my new place for a meet and greet!" She let out a squeal. "It's starting . . . right now."

She zoomed out on the camera, and my mouth dropped open.

She was standing outside of Jackson's place.

"You've got to be kidding me . . ." Jackson muttered as he straightened.

He grabbed his radio to call backup.

Before he could, Fake Joey rattled off his address.

Then she smiled at the camera as she said, "I look forward to seeing you all here."

CHAPTER
FOURTEEN

BY THE TIME officers got to Jackson's house, Fake Joey was gone.

But eighty-some people had gathered outside, crowding the place and waiting for me to emerge.

Jackson had stayed at the police station with me, monitoring the situation from there.

I was more worried about Ripley, but apparently the dog was okay.

That was good news, at least.

The rest of the afternoon had stretched on longer than I wanted, and I knew it wasn't safe for me to either go back to my new house or to Jackson's old place.

Not now that this woman had announced Jackson's address to anyone who might be watching.

That wasn't cool.

As I sat in Jackson's office returning several text messages from my manager, I considered reporter Amanda's offer again.

Maybe it *would* be a good idea for me to come clean to all my fans about what was happening. I was already breaking news. People were going to be confused, and the only person who'd be painted in a bad light was me. Fake Joey would, most likely, disappear from sight and leave me to clean up the crime scene she'd created.

I knew the way this worked.

Jackson strode back into his office—he'd been talking with some of his colleagues—that scowl still on his face. "I talked to Phoebe, and she said we could stay with her as long as we need to. That's the only solution I can think of."

"Good plan. I don't want to go back to your place either."

"That fake Joey woman has some nerve." He shook his head, clearly still upset.

"I agree. This whole situation is making me more and more uncomfortable."

He shifted in front of me, his thoughts seeming to switch gears. "Are you still considering Amanda's offer?"

I let out a breath. "Maybe. Or maybe I don't need to go through her. I mean, if she interviewed me, I still wouldn't be controlling the narrative because she could edit the story to make it whatever she wants. Maybe I'll take this situation into my own hands. But I want to think about it more first."

He nodded and grabbed his keys from his pocket. "I'm all done here. How about if we head to Phoebe's? We can stop by our place to grab some clothes in the meantime."

"That sounds good."

So we did just that. Thankfully, no one had showed up there. I halfway expected a crowd to emerge out of the woodwork, almost like in that movie *Small Soldiers*. Maybe it was part of this woman's evil little plan to demolish any peace of mind I had.

As we climbed back into Jackson's truck with Ripley, one more idea popped into my head—something we needed to do before we headed down to Hatteras Island, where Phoebe lived.

"Would you mind if we got some ice cream at Sprinkles?" I asked.

He shrugged. "I guess ice cream always cheers people up."

It did. And I really *did* want ice cream.

Of course, I had ulterior motives, but I wasn't sure this was the best time to bring them up to Jackson.

We wove through traffic and ten minutes later arrived at the ice cream place. It was a cute little building that had once been a gas station. Now, the exterior was painted white, and colorful "sprinkles" decorated the signage around the glass doors.

A line of customers already crept out the door.

The owner was no doubt thrilled with this place's popularity. Businesses around here had to make most of their profit during the summer months because the winter could practically be dead.

From what I'd heard, the seasons weren't as drastic as they used to be. More and more people were beginning to visit during the winter months. But it was still like a different place around here during cold weather.

Jackson, Ripley, and I all got in line.

As usual, I pulled on my hat and sunglasses. I couldn't handle any more attention right now.

"What are you thinking about?" Jackson leaned closer and whispered in my ear.

His warm breath sent tingles down my spine, and I had to resist the urge to lean into him.

I had to force my thoughts onto something other than his touch.

"I'm thinking about . . . the fact that all those people showed up for a meet and greet with me, only to be stood up." I frowned. "It makes me look bad."

"You could explain things."

Yes, I could. In fact, it appeared my hand was being forced here.

I could only imagine the angry comments people would post online about me because of this.

Just what was Fake Joey's end goal? I couldn't figure that out.

And who was the man she'd met with when she slipped out the back of the grocery store?

So many questions went through my mind.

Finally, we reached the counter to order. I got two scoops of double chocolate fudge ice cream, and Jackson got a strawberry milkshake.

We found a table in the corner to enjoy our treats—most people went to the bright yellow picnic tables outside. I needed to be close if I was going to talk to Frank.

I watched him now as he wiped down tables.

Finally, he made his way to mine.

"Fancy seeing you two here," he started as he nodded at me then Jackson.

Just as earlier, he seemed nervous.

"Frank . . ." I started, hoping my ice cream didn't melt all over my hands. "I came here to see you, actually."

His skin grew paler. "Why would you do that? Should I be flattered?"

"You know something about my dad, don't you?" Again, I dove in without checking the water depth.

He continued wiping down the table beside me. "I don't know what you're talking about."

"Frank . . . I can tell by your face that you're hiding something." Sure enough, chocolate ice cream dripped down my fingers.

Jackson handed me some napkins to clean up my mess, but his look clearly said I should have gotten a milkshake like him.

Frank shrugged, avoiding eye contact. "It's nothing."

"If it's nothing, tell me."

He glanced at me and paused. He quickly scanned the ice cream shop before stepping closer. "Your dad asked me to keep an eye on you, okay?"

My heart beat harder. "He did. When?"

"Right before he disappeared the second time. It was almost like he knew he was going to have to vanish again, but he was worried about something."

My pulse quickened. "Did he say anything else?"

Frank pressed his lips together before saying, "Lew said he discovered something that he couldn't tell anyone."

Something he couldn't tell anyone? Not even me? After everything we'd been through with my mom?

She'd been gone from my life for so many years

only to reappear in an old photo my dad had in his belongings. The problem was that the photo hadn't been old. It had been recent.

Then she showed up and saved my life, only to vanish again. Then I was told that she was possibly involved with the Barracudas. When the group had been busted, she hadn't been with them. Since then, she'd been in the wind.

Meanwhile, my dad had been an informant for the DEA after he discovered a "friend" who worked at the docks was doing some shady deals.

Everything was so complicated, and none of us had very long to chat during that final confrontation. I didn't have all the answers I wanted, but I'd tried to be okay with that.

Clearly, I wasn't okay.

Had my dad discovered something he hadn't even told me about? Was there more to the story than I had ever realized?

I didn't know.

But I did know that doubt about this whole situation was beginning to mess with my mind.

And when I glanced at my ice cream cone again, I realized most of it was now a chocolate puddle on the table.

Once we arrived at Phoebe's place, I decided to make a video statement for my fans.

The primary reason I wanted to do so was to ensure my fans didn't get conned. I mean, what if Fake Joey started asking people for money or favors using my name and influence? What if, like Jackson had said, she used my name to lure men into doing her lurid deeds?

Not only would that paint me in a bad light, but I also didn't want my fans to experience that kind of betrayal.

So it was time for me to be proactive.

I called Amanda and told her my decision. She argued with me and begged for me to let her do this story.

I politely told her I wouldn't change my mind.

Then I set up my phone on the top deck of Phoebe's place where the beautiful Pamlico Sound would be displayed behind me. Phoebe, Jackson, and Ripley stood in front of me as I began my statement.

"Hello, everyone! I wish I was coming on here with some fun update." I frowned. "But I'm not. I'll just dive right into the heart of the matter. It's come to my attention that there's a woman in the Outer Banks who's impersonating me."

I paused as I gave people time to digest that.

"This woman looks eerily similar to me," I

continued a few seconds later. "She even talks like me and acts like me. This woman is making videos and public appearances where she claims to be me. But I'm here to let you know that she is not me."

I paused once more and took a long drink of my water. This was a lot for people to process.

"I want you to know that I'll never ask any of you for money or any type of favors. So if you see a video of me or read something online saying that's what I need, don't believe it. I would never do that."

I drew in a deep breath. This was harder than I'd anticipated.

"Just to let you know, I'm working with the local police so we can come to a resolution about what's going on and locate this woman. In the meantime, if you see anything online, and if it's not from my social media handle with the verified blue checkmark beside it, it's not me. I urge you to remain cautious. I do love and care about all of you. I'm sorry for any turmoil this may have caused you. I'll give you updates when I can. Peace out."

I hit End on my phone and then relaxed my shoulders slightly. I glanced at Jackson and Phoebe.

Jackson gave me a thumbs-up. "Well said."

"I'm going to type something up also and put it out there for anybody who may not want to watch this video."

"Are you ready to unwind for the evening?" Jackson asked.

I started to tell him yes when my phone rang.

I recognized the number right away.

It was Fake Dad.

CHAPTER
FIFTEEN

I PUT the phone on speaker as I answered.

"Hello?" I glanced at Jackson and then Phoebe to make sure they were listening.

They were.

"Joey . . ." Fake Dad started, an edge of caution in his voice. "I just saw the video you posted."

"That was quick." I swatted away a mosquito a little too fervently—probably because it wasn't the mosquitos that bothered me. It was this whole situation, but I was taking out my frustration on the little bloodsuckers around me.

"I've been concerned ever since you told me the woman I met wasn't really you. Since then, I've been monitoring the internet for any new developments. That was really you this time, right?"

"It was."

"I saw the other video she posted that sent people to your house. I'm sorry you're going through all this."

I had to admit that the man sounded sincere and concerned. I didn't know what to think about that.

I didn't want his fatherly compassion to play on my emotions. I needed to keep my walls up until I knew if this man was safe. Right now, my gut indicated he wasn't.

In fact, I didn't *want* him to be safe.

After all, he wasn't my dad. It just wasn't even a possibility.

"I was wondering if you might be interested in meeting tomorrow for breakfast," he said.

I glanced at Jackson again, and his gaze held mine as he waited for my response. He was leaving the ball in my court, which I appreciated.

I nibbled on my lip as I considered my options.

Then I nodded. "Okay. But only if my husband can come with me."

I looked at Jackson, and he nodded his approval.

"Of course. Where would you like to meet? You can pick."

I rattled off the name of the restaurant, and we agreed to be there tomorrow morning at eight.

I already felt the thrum of nerves inside me, however.

Because I had no idea what that conversation would hold.

But perhaps my biggest fear was . . . what if this man somehow proved that he really was my biological dad?

If that happened, how would I ever come to terms with that truth?

Joey . . . I am your father.

Those words still rang in my ears, still sounding like Darth Vader.

And just like in the Star Wars movies, I kind of felt like I was facing off with evil. Like the fate of the world depended on me defeating the Galactic Empire.

The fate of my world, at least.

Those were the thoughts running through my head the next morning as Jackson and I sat at a corner table at The Egg Bistro.

My normal breakfast haunts were either Sunrise Coffee Company or Oh Buoy. But I decided it would be better to go somewhere this morning where I wasn't known.

And I *had* heard this place was delicious.

Ripley had been able to stay at Phoebe's, which

worked out well. I only prayed that Fake Joey didn't somehow catch wind of where I was staying now and try to send fans that way also.

My stomach clenched at the thought of it.

What an invasion of privacy.

Jackson squeezed my hand as he sat beside me at a table along the back wall. The scents of bacon and sausage drifted around us, making my stomach grumble. I hadn't had bacon in so long, and it seemed like a great comfort food right now.

"You don't have to do this," Jackson told me.

I swallowed hard. "I know. But if I don't get some answers, then it's going to bug me. It's better just to get this over with."

Jackson nodded.

Just then, Fake Dad stepped into the restaurant. Paused near the door. Glanced around. Then he spotted me.

With a tentative smile, he strode toward me and Jackson.

I stared at him as he approached.

Was this guy really a spy? He was tall, which would make it harder for him to blend in. Didn't spies want to blend in? Or was that just a TV thing?

I really had no idea. To my detriment, my reality was grounded in Hollywood.

Should I stand as he approached us?

I wasn't sure, but I didn't.

He started to reach out his hand toward Jackson, but then seemed to think better of it when my husband gave him an icy stare.

Instead, Adolf—I still cringed at that name—pulled out a chair and sat down. "Thank you for meeting with me."

"Of course." I pushed a laminated menu toward him. "I hear the food is delicious. Why don't we order something before we start talking?"

The truth was that I wasn't certain I'd be able to eat anything, but I knew I should probably try.

That's why a few minutes later, I ordered a veggie omelet with fruit on the side as well as a refill on my coffee. Jackson got the Big Breakfast plate—bacon, two scrambled eggs, hashbrowns, and grits. And Fake Dad ordered red velvet waffles.

When that was done, I realized I had nothing else to delay this conversation and had no choice but to talk.

I waited for Fake Dad to begin.

CHAPTER
SIXTEEN

"SO . . ." I wiggled my fingers in and out of each other as my hands rested on the table, a nervous habit.

Eric used to always call me Octopus Fingers when I did that—as an insult, not as an affectionate nickname.

I was still working through some of the baggage that came from that toxic relationship. I feared it would take me years of counseling. I'd already been through a lot of therapy, and I was in a much better place.

"I'm not even sure what to say," I finally admitted as I cupped my hands around my coffee mug. "You wanted to meet?"

Fake Dad shifted in his seat, the lines on his face

seeming deeper today than they had when we first met. "I know this is awkward. I appreciate you giving me another chance."

"Has the other Joey contacted you anymore?" Jackson didn't look at all awkward—only anxious for answers.

I could appreciate that.

Adolf shook his head. "No. I mean, it was *you* I talked to on the phone last night, right? This is the real Joey Darling I'm sitting across from right now?"

I tilted my head to the side, realizing how strange this conversation was. "You really can't tell the difference between us?"

He shrugged. "The similarities *are* striking."

I couldn't argue with that. I supposed if someone didn't know me that well, it could be confusing.

"I have something I think might clear up some of your questions." Fake Dad reached into the back pocket of his khaki cargo shorts and then slid a black-and-white photo across the table.

I blinked several times as I picked it up and stared at the images there.

My mom was clearly in the photo. Mom with her five-foot-nine slim figure. Her long, dark hair. Her classic features.

She'd once been Miss Apple Blossom. Had pursued modeling.

I got my looks from her—but I didn't even come close to her beauty.

She was stunning with those high cheekbones, big eyes, and full lips.

My gaze traveled to the person in the photo with her.

I sucked in a breath.

That was clearly Fake Dad standing beside her. He was much younger in the photo, though. At least thirty years.

Their arms were around each other, and a cobblestone path led to a castle in the background.

A castle?

I'd guess this photo was taken somewhere in Europe, which may or may not confirm his claim that he'd been a spy.

Despite the defensiveness rising inside me, I couldn't deny what I was seeing right now.

"How do I know this wasn't photoshopped?" I stared at Fake Dad, looking for any signs of deceit.

I saw none. No averted gaze. No shifting in his seat. No fidgeting.

Then again, spies were good at subterfuge.

"You don't." His cheek twitched as if he fought a frown. "Nothing I can say will convince you the photo is authentic. But it is. Your mother and I . . . we were madly in love."

I stared at the picture again and frowned. "How did you know my mom?"

At least, I could settle on that truth. If this photo was real, they *had* known each other.

"I was working an assignment in Austria, and she was one of my assets. We became close and fell in love. Then she decided she wanted out of that line of work. She wanted a more normal life—much like you when you decided to move from Hollywood."

I raised an eyebrow. "You know about that?"

He offered a quick nod. "I do. I've been following your career."

His words caused my cheeks to flush, though I wasn't sure why. "Go on. Tell me more about my mom."

Fake Dad's gaze clouded with memories. "Melinda begged me to come with her, but I couldn't. I had too much on the line. Let's face it, I loved my job too much. But she came back to the States, where she met your father."

"That must have been difficult for you."

He shrugged. "It was. But I understood. A month later, they were married. Eight months later, you were born."

I shook my head. My dad had told me once that he and mother fell in love quickly. That when you knew a person was the one, you knew. That's why they'd married without knowing each other that well.

There was just enough truth in Fake Dad's story to give me a moment of doubt.

Right then, our food was delivered. I was grateful for something to distract me.

After lifting a silent prayer, I picked up my fork and used the edge to cut into my omelet—even though my appetite was gone.

I drew in a deep breath before asking, "When was the last time you talked to my mom?"

Adolf didn't answer right away. Instead, the question hung in the air.

That made me even more anxious to hear the answer.

Adolf shifted in his seat. "I talked to Melinda a few years ago."

I raised my eyebrows as my heart began to pound faster. "Why? Was it your idea or hers? Did you talk on the phone? Or did you see her in person?"

He raised a hand as if to encourage me to slow down my questions. "We met in DC. She found me and approached me as I headed to my apartment."

"Why?"

"She found herself in the middle of a tricky situation and needed my help."

I swallowed before saying, "I'm going to need more details than that."

Fake Dad frowned. "I'm afraid I can't share more details than that. It's . . . well, it's classified."

"You're saying that Joey's mom is still doing classified work? Even though she wanted out of it?" Jackson leaned closer as if he couldn't believe this man's statement either.

Jackson had barely touched his breakfast, which showed he was distracted by this conversation as well.

"It's complicated." Adolf frowned and glanced at his untouched waffles. "I know that seems like a cop-out. But when you're in my line of business, it's the truth."

I swallowed hard as I tried to figure out what to ask next.

I finally settled on, "Have you talked to my mom since then?"

"No."

"Do you know where she is now?"

"No, I'm sorry. I don't. She's very good at remaining hidden."

"Yes, she is." Jackson narrowed his eyes. "She'd be in prison right now if she wasn't."

She'd disappeared during the sting where other members of the terrorist group had been arrested. Jackson had been there, and I could tell it still bothered him.

Finally, I got to my bottom line and locked gazes with Fake Dad. "Why are you here now? What do you want from me?"

A frown pulled at the sides of his lips. "Nothing. Just to get to know you."

"Do you know that other woman?" Jackson's gaze bore into Adolf's. "The other Joey?"

Again, I stared at Adolf, wanting to see the truth in his eyes. Just as before, he didn't blink or look away.

"No, I promise," Fake Dad said. "I don't."

Jackson's phone rang, and he stepped away to take the call. When he came back only seconds later, his expression looked grim.

"I hate to cut this short, but I can't stay any longer." His gaze locked with mine. "Joey, I'd really like it if you would come with me."

I stood, not sure if I was relieved or disappointed to end this conversation.

Adolf pulled out his wallet. "This is on me. I'm still in town for a few more days. Let me know if you would like to meet again."

Did I want to meet again?

I wasn't sure.

CHAPTER
SEVENTEEN

"I DON'T WANT to alarm you," Jackson said as we climbed into his SUV. "But you know that random burst of gunfire that happened outside our place?"

"Hard to forget it." I flinched as I remembered being rocked from my peaceful evening at that horrible sound.

"It just happened again."

I sucked in a breath as I pulled my seatbelt on. "What? Where?"

"Near Whispering Sands Street."

I gasped. "That's where Beach Combers is! Have you talked to Dizzy? Is she okay? Was anyone hurt?"

"Dizzy is fine. This just happened, so we're still trying to gather the rest of the details." He turned on his police lights and siren before speeding down the road toward the scene.

My heart and thoughts raced along with the vehicle. "Do you think someone took out a hit on her?"

As soon as the question left my lips, I realized what I'd said.

Jackson slowly slid his eyes toward me before glancing back at the road. "Why would you think this is a hit?"

I frowned and said nothing. Anything I said could and would be used against me. I knew that from experience.

"Joey . . ." Jackson's voice hardened. "Start talking."

I sighed, wondering why I was delaying the inevitable. More time passing wouldn't make this any less painful.

"I . . . *may* have run into someone who told me there's a hit out on somebody."

"Who?" Jackson didn't hide his irritation.

I remained quiet.

"It was Danny, wasn't it?" Jackson finally asked over the whine of the siren.

Again, I said nothing. I didn't have to.

Jackson knew the truth. But I really didn't want to get Danny in trouble. That hadn't been my intention.

"Joey . . ." Jackson sighed as he stared at the road ahead. "This was supposed to be under wraps."

"I was just worried about whatever was going on . . ."

"You should've waited for me to tell you." Jackson sounded mad—like, really mad.

"I'm sorry," I finally murmured, feeling a tremble claim my arms.

I knew I still had a lot of growing to do.

I didn't like fighting with Jackson. But I also didn't like being in the dark.

I wanted more than anything to have a healthy relationship with him, especially since my first marriage had been such a disaster. I was determined not to let the past repeat itself now that Jackson and I had tied the knot.

But it seemed like at every turn, I failed.

I cast those thoughts aside as we pulled up at Dizzy's place. I knew Jackson and I would need to address this conversation again later.

But, for now, I had to see for myself that my aunt was okay.

As soon as I got out of the car, I spotted Dizzy on the other side of the police barricade and ran toward her.

When I reached her, I threw my arms around her neck.

Other than Jackson and my dad, Dizzy was my only other *real* family. The thought of losing her . . .

Tears welled in my eyes.

I didn't think I could handle losing anyone else in my life.

"Are you okay?" I put my hands on her shoulders as I stepped back to look her in the eyes.

White powder—probably plaster—covered her face, and her red lipstick was smeared as well as her mascara. She had that stunned look in her eyes, and her motions seemed stiff.

I rarely saw my feisty aunt in this state.

Finally, she nodded. "I'm fine. Just shaken. Thankfully, I'd just gotten back from my break, so no one was in the salon."

"I'm so glad. I was *so* worried when I heard what had happened."

We both turned to look at her shop.

The place was an old, one-story beach house that had been converted to a business. The cedar shingles had been painted bright pink, and a hand-painted sign proclaimed "Beach Combers Hair Salon" to everyone who passed.

Now, the front windows were broken, and several bullet holes marred the exterior walls.

"Why would someone do this?" Dizzy rubbed her arms as if she were chilled despite the heat outside. "It just doesn't make sense."

"It really doesn't. Hopefully, the police will catch these guys."

Behind me, I heard Jackson talking to some of his colleagues. "What's this guy's pattern? He *has* to have a target."

"Maybe. We know someone else is behind this, the one pulling the strings and footing the bill. Maybe that's what we need to focus on."

Jackson sighed. "Without more details, that's proving to be difficult."

There was one thing I knew for sure. Fake Dad hadn't been the one who pulled the trigger. He'd been with me and Jackson, so he had an alibi.

But . . . what if Adolf had coordinated our breakfast with this shooting just to throw us off-balance? What if he was the one pulling the strings and paying for these drive-by shootings?

There was so much I didn't know.

I glanced up as a news van swerved onto the scene.

Of *course* the news had shown up. They always did.

They must have been close to get here this soon.

Then I saw . . . Amanda step out.

Dread filled me. *She* was the reporter handling the story?

I frowned.

That was just great.

CHAPTER
EIGHTEEN

I SENSED Amanda glancing at me while trying to interview various police officers who refused to make any statements.

Still, she kept her microphone on hand to update her viewers as her cameraman got footage of the broken windows from outside Dizzy's shop.

I doubted if this was breaking news, so I could only assume they were filming this for later.

Then the dreaded moment I'd been anticipating happened.

Amanda must have assumed she wouldn't get any information from anyone on the scene of the shooting, so she moseyed up to me instead.

I now stood on the other side of the police line. Dizzy was talking to the police chief, who'd also shown up.

"If it isn't Joey Darling." Something close to a hopeful smirk tugged at Amanda's lips—a hopeful smirk surrounded by desperate ambition. "Fancy seeing you here. But are you really Joey?"

I scowled. "Very funny."

Her smile disappeared. "I know this isn't funny. And I *am* sorry you're going through this. I can only imagine how frustrating it might be."

"You can say that again."

I almost told her that I'd gotten arrested when the police had thought I was Fake Joey, but I knew that would probably end up on the news, so I kept quiet. I didn't want the negative attention.

"I saw the post you did online." Her voice sounded subtly accusatory. "I guess you didn't want me breaking the news, huh?"

"I need to be able to control this narrative before the facts get muddled by other people." I really didn't have to explain myself to her, yet I found myself doing so anyway.

"You could've trusted me." Her chin nudged out.

"Why would I do that? I don't know you. I have no reason to trust you. I understand that you want to get ahead and that you're trying to build a career. I can sympathize with that. But this is my life we're talking about, not just a stepping stone in your career."

She frowned and looked away as if she understood, even if she wouldn't admit it.

Then she looked back at me as if she'd recalculated. "We could still do something, you know. My producer is pushing me to put something together."

"I'm sorry you're being pressured. It's especially a bummer because he's pressuring you to do something that you have no control over."

Her eyes narrowed, and her lips puckered with irritation. "He told me I need to convince you. No matter what it takes."

"Unfortunately, I'm not a machine that you can switch on and off. I can't be controlled." Lesson 547 that I'd learned after being with Eric and the therapy sessions that had followed.

Amanda frowned and looked away again. I knew she was trying to come up with another tactic that might convince me to say yes.

It wasn't going to work.

Jackson stepped up to us just then, and I'd never been so grateful for his presence.

"Everything okay here?" Jackson's perceptive gaze bounced between the two of us.

"Just peachy," I told him.

"Hey, you guys." The cameraman stepped into our circle. "There's a new video of the other Joey."

The other Joey? I narrowed my eyes. This woman was not the other me.

He held up his phone, and we all began watching.

Fake Joey was filming herself again, an unidentifiable blank white wall behind her. Smart on her part.

"Someone professing to be me posted a video yesterday claiming that nothing I've said is true." Fake Joey flashed a pouty frown at the camera. "That's just not accurate."

"What?" This girl . . . she was really getting under my skin.

"I'm not sure why someone's pretending to be me," Fake Joey continued, sounding like a victim. "And such a downer version of me too."

My mouth dropped open. "I'm not a downer!"

"It's a shame that the world has come to this," Fake Joey said. "But I'm here to let you know that *I* am the real Joey Darling. I truly do love my fans. I can't wait to show you guys just how much I love and appreciate you. So stay tuned to this account to hear more of the inside scoop. *Ciao!*"

As her words hung in the air, I noticed Jackson, Amanda, and the cameraman were staring at me.

"She's got you down pat." Amanda shrugged. "I mean, it's eerie."

My scowl deepened. "I know."

I didn't mean to sound so terse, but how could I

not? What initially seemed as if it could potentially be an innocent joke was turning out to be anything but.

What would this woman do next? Try to take over my life? Invade my home, and pretend to be me to see if Jackson would notice?

How far would she go?

What if she killed me in order to take over my life?

I rubbed my arms. Okay, that sounded extreme. Maybe I'd watched one too many thrillers.

But what if it wasn't my TV viewing habits influencing those thoughts? What if this woman really was psycho?

That was a question that I couldn't get out of my head.

I stayed at the scene another thirty minutes and managed to avoid any more conversations with Amanda.

Thankfully, a police spokesperson had come out to make a statement and had occupied the reporter's time. Meanwhile, Dizzy was free to leave, and Jackson asked if I would go with her.

There was really nothing else I could do here, and

spending some time with my aunt seemed like a good option.

We pulled up to her place a few minutes later.

She lived in a small cottage on the sound side of the island in a neighborhood mostly filled with full-time locals. The area was a refreshing change from the rows and rows of rental houses on stilts comprising most of the island. These streets contained halfway normal homes with swing sets and flowerbeds.

The inside fit Dizzy perfectly—bright-blue walls, purple accessories, and boas instead of curtains.

She fixed us some tea and then we sat at her kitchen table to talk.

I filled her in on the conversation I'd had today with Frank—including the fact that my dad asked him to keep an eye on me before he'd disappeared. I also told Dizzy that my dad told Frank he'd discovered something that he couldn't tell anyone.

"That doesn't sound like your father!" Dizzy narrowed her eyes protectively.

"That's what I thought too. The only reason he'd keep a secret would be to . . . protect someone." I took a sip of my tea.

She tilted her head. "To protect *you*."

I let out a sigh. She was absolutely right.

"Did Uncle Hugh ever say anything about this?" Dizzy's husband had been a kind man—and quiet. The two had definitely balanced each other that way.

He and my father had been best friends as well as brothers.

Dizzy let out a long breath before shaking her head. "No, if any of this is true—and I don't think it is—then your uncle knew nothing about it. There's just no way. I would've known if he had a secret he was keeping from me. I could read that man like a book."

Unless my dad kept it a secret from him also.

I really thought the two of them shared every-thing—even a girlfriend once, though not on purpose. The two of them used to have a good laugh about how a girl in high school had pulled the wool over both their eyes.

I licked my lips, my throat tightening as I prepared to ask my next question. If anyone knew the answer, it would be Dizzy. "Is there any chance . . . that . . . I could have . . . a twin?"

I flinched after I asked the question, knowing I would sound crazy.

"A twin?" Dizzy fanned her face. "Why would you think that? You think that girl is actually your sister?"

"I don't know. I don't know anything!" My words came out a little too fast. "I'm just trying to think of possible explanations!"

Dizzy pressed her lips together before leaning closer. "You weren't a twin. I was there when you were born."

I let out the breath that I didn't realize I'd been holding. "Okay, at least I can mark that off my list of possibilities."

"I have one more thought." Dizzy took a sip of her tea. "Is there any way that you could contact your dad and talk to him right now?"

I had thought about that also. "I'm only supposed to talk to him in case of an emergency."

"What constitutes an emergency?"

"Something that's life or death, I guess." I shrugged.

"This isn't life or death?" Dizzy stared at me, her eyes wide.

"I'm . . . not sure."

"Well, who would you contact if that was the case?"

"There was a marshal named Ted Manson, who worked with my father when he went undercover as an informant for the DEA."

"Do you know how to get in touch with him?"

"I don't . . . but Jackson does."

But I'd have to think long and hard before I went that route.

CHAPTER
NINETEEN

JACKSON PICKED me up two hours later.

Dizzy had curled my hair, giving me beach waves. She'd painted my nails purple. She'd wanted to do my makeup also, but I'd stopped her.

The last time she'd done that, I had blue eye shadow up to my eyebrows. Unfortunately, it had become a trend when someone saw it online, and—under the instruction of my manager—I'd been forced to wear the shade for the next few months.

This was what happened when you needed to pass time with a beautician.

But I had to admit that the distraction had been nice.

As excitement lit Jackson's gaze, I sensed there was something he wanted to tell me.

"What's going on?" I asked. "Did you catch the person who shot at us?"

"No, I didn't. We're still working on that."

"Then why do you look like a little boy who just got his first love note?"

"After we left The Egg Bistro, I had a plain clothes officer stationed outside who followed your fake dad."

What? Why hadn't he told me?

As if he read my thoughts, he said, "I was afraid if I told you, it would show all over your face."

"But I'm an actress!"

"We didn't have time for a take two on this one. I don't know how much this is affecting you emotionally."

I frowned. He spoke the truth. I was a tad bit emotional about all this.

"Well . . . that was brilliant." I partially scolded myself for not thinking of it on my own. "So you know where he is right now?"

"I know where he's staying. But my officer couldn't stick around because this isn't officially part of our police investigation. I thought we might just want to drive past and see if we notice anything."

I leaned over and kissed him on the cheek. "You're brilliant. Did I mention that yet?"

"You did, but feel free to keep saying it."

We headed down the road toward Southern Shores, a town located on the northern side of Outer Banks.

Once we got closer, Jackson cut over to the beach road.

"His house is right up there." He pointed to a two-story oceanfront rental in the distance, one with a car parked in front of it.

We stopped at a light, and I looked at the place, wondering if I would be able to tell any details about Fake Dad just from looking at the outside.

I couldn't.

Jackson found a parking space in front of a small tourist shop. Then we crossed to the beach to observe the house from the other side of the dunes. Thankfully, the sand wasn't too high right here, which gave us a decent view.

"We're doing a stakeout, aren't we?" I asked as Jackson and I strolled the beach slowly, trying not to be too obvious.

"I suppose we are."

I looped my arm through his. "This is so exciting!"

He chuckled. "I'm glad you like it, Joey."

We paced a good distance down the shore before turning and heading back.

My gaze remained on the house as we walked.

A movement on the first floor caught my eye.

A man was being escorted out a sliding glass door by two burly, unsmiling men.

They held onto his arms as they took him down the porch steps.

"Jackson . . ."

He tensed beside me.

"That's him. But who are those guys?" I muttered. "Why are they holding onto Adolf?"

"Stay here." Jackson didn't wait for my response as he took off, his phone to his ear.

But before he even reached the dune, the men stuffed Fake Dad into a black SUV and took off.

Jackson paused atop the dune and scowled. He shoved his phone back into his pocket and motioned to me.

I quickly caught up to him.

"By the time we get back to the SUV, they'll be long gone," he explained.

"So what do we do?"

"My guys on patrol will look for that SUV. I need to search the inside of this place and see if there's any evidence of what's going on."

Jackson searched the house, but there were nearly no personal belongings—only clothes and toiletries.

Which didn't really surprise me, unfortunately.

Fake Dad was clever. If he really had been CIA, then he'd learned to cover his tracks.

But I couldn't get the image of Fake Dad being abducted out of my mind.

I didn't know the guy, and I didn't even necessarily like him.

But whatever was happening was serious.

After searching for nearly an hour, Jackson and I went back to the police station. I'd done a little snooping on my own, but I hadn't discovered anything either. I was more than a little disappointed.

Thankfully, the police chief and the mayor both loved me. When I first moved to this area, I'd tried to give the department all the good press I could by doing a series of tweets with the hashtag: NHPDBlues. They'd been a hit.

At my suggestion, the men at the station had even done a calendar to raise money for the Fraternal Order of Police. I'd posted about it on social media, and as a result they'd raised more than two hundred thousand dollars for their police charity. Jackson, of course, had been the star of the calendar—in my humble opinion. I still had his picture from the calendar on my desk.

Jackson and the chief allowed me into the conference room as the two of them talked, along with two other detectives and a couple of officers.

"Was anyone able to run the plates?" Jackson asked.

"I was." One of the officers who had a laptop in front of him raised a finger in the air to draw attention to himself. "I fully expected it to be a rental or stolen."

"But . . ." Jackson stared at him.

"Just give me a minute here . . ." The officer leaned toward his computer. "The car is actually owned by someone named Grayson Wright. At first glance, it looks like Grayson lives in Virginia and works for the Department of Defense as an engineer."

"Okay . . ." Jackson waited, but I could hear the testiness in his voice.

"Like I said, on the surface, Grayson seems like a stand-up guy. I mean, he even has a top-level security clearance, right? But digging deeper, I was able to figure out he's also on a watch list."

"What kind of watch list?" Now the officer had Jackson's full attention.

Mine too.

"It turns out, he gave a considerable sum of

money to a man named Dietrich Baklava. But that transaction ended up getting flagged."

"Why is that?" the chief asked.

"Dietrich . . . has ties with the Russian mafia."

Jackson let out a breath. "So, since the car hasn't been reported stolen, we can assume that the Russians borrowed this guy's car and used it to snatch Adolf?"

My hand flew over my mouth as Jackson's words settled on me.

What if Fake Dad wasn't CIA, and he was really a Russian spy?

CHAPTER
TWENTY

I COULD HARDLY CONTAIN my impatience as things unfolded at the police station over the next couple of hours. The chief had given me permission to sit in.

The police were in touch with the rental agency that took care of the house where Adolf was staying. He'd registered under the name Adolf Faulkner.

However, Adolf Faulkner did not exist.

He had paid with cash and put a security deposit down with a credit card—however, it was a prepaid credit card, so that led police nowhere.

He'd also had to provide a copy of his driver's license to the management company.

They listed his home address in Northern Virginia, and no one by his name lived at that actual address.

All in all, it became apparent that Adolf was using an alias, and that he was good at the whole subterfuge thing spies were supposed to be good at.

I wanted to sit down and talk to Jackson, to hash through some theories.

But he was in and out of the room as he ran down leads and got updates from people.

Despite everything happening, the cops still hadn't found the abductors' vehicle, nor had they found the person responsible for the random drive-by shootings.

It wasn't that these officers and detectives were incompetent. They really weren't.

The fact of the matter was that the perpetrators of these crimes were skilled and had multiple resources at their disposal.

Finally, Jackson joined me and told me he was going to take me back to Phoebe's for the night.

That was fine with me. It had been a long day, and I was tired.

Plus, I needed to talk to my manager to see if he could get Fake Joey's social media accounts suspended.

Phoebe wasn't home when we got back to her place. I vaguely remembered her saying she was meeting with a client for her dog-sitting business.

Jackson and I made ourselves at home, just as Phoebe had told us to. Jackson let Ripley run around outside on the shore for a while. There was nothing that dog liked better.

By the time they came back inside, I'd ordered pizza for Jackson from a nearby restaurant and a grilled chicken salad for myself.

We sat at the table across from each other, and I stared at Jackson, trying to read his expression.

"Any updates on finding Fake Joey?"

Jackson took a bite of his double pepperoni pizza slice and shook his head. After he swallowed, he said, "No, it's weird because she's so public and so well hidden."

"I know . . . it is weird." I pushed my food around on my plate, knowing I should eat yet having so much on my mind . . . "I can't help but wonder if all three of these things are connected."

"All three things being the fake Joey, your fake dad, and the drive-by shootings?"

I nodded. "I mean, I know it's a stretch, but they all seemed to happen at the same time."

"Maybe. But I don't see where the drive-by shootings could be connected. Other than the fact that our house was hit. But that also seems like it was random. We're not even sure if they have a specific target. They could just want to cause terror in the area. If so, it's working. We've had people canceling their vacation reservations."

"I honestly don't blame them." I let out a breath. "Do you think the men who abducted my fake dad could be connected with the hitman?"

"Not that we know of."

"And we don't know who hired this hitman, so this person could be hiding in plain sight?"

"That's a possibility."

Finally, I put down my fork and ran a hand through my hair. "This is just too much."

Jackson reached across the table and squeezed my hand. "I know it's a lot. Why don't you go get changed, and we can watch a movie or something? It would be good for you to have something to take your mind off all of this."

I nodded. "I like that idea."

I was getting a headache, and sometimes my best ideas came to me when I wasn't trying so hard.

I sighed and wandered into my temporary bedroom.

I paused by the bed and glanced down. I hadn't come into the room since I'd gotten back.

A folded piece of paper sat on the comforter.

Had Phoebe left us a note telling us where she was going?

Interesting. She was usually more of the texting type.

I snatched it off the bed.

The words I read caused my lungs to freeze.

Not everyone is as they seem were the simple words scrawled on the beige cardstock.

What was even more eerie was the fact that the writing almost resembled . . . my mom's.

JACKSON HAD CHECKED the note for fingerprints.

He found none.

Then he'd gone next door to the neighbors to ask if they'd seen anyone lurking around the house.

They hadn't.

He paused beside me in the living room. "You really think that's your mom's writing?"

I let out a sigh before shrugging. "I mean, it's hard to know for sure. But I have a couple of cards she sent me for my birthday when I was younger. She leaves a very firm impression with her pen, and her cursive is loopy. This is . . . it's very similar."

"I don't like this."

"At least . . . I don't think . . . I mean, I don't know but . . . I don't think my mom wants to hurt me."

"No, this person seems to want to warn you. But breaking into the residence where you're staying isn't the way to do it."

I couldn't argue.

Jackson stormed to Phoebe's laptop, grabbed it, and brought it to the kitchen table. He'd helped set up the security system and still had the information to monitor it—Phoebe had given him permission, of course.

He found the website so he could check Phoebe's cameras on the outside of the house. There were only two. One in the front and one in the back.

I sat beside him as he began to study the video footage. Jackson found the moment when Phoebe had left the house two hours before we arrived.

"I can only assume that someone left a note while she was here, and maybe the doors were unlocked."

Jackson continued to scan the rest of the footage, speeding through the reel to save time.

He paused at one point and rewound it.

I sat up straighter. "Did you see something?"

"I'm not sure yet." He hit the Play button again and reduced it to the normal speed.

Forty seconds later, the screen went black.

"What?" I couldn't believe what I was seeing. "How long was it out?"

"Good question." He forwarded the video until it came back on ten minutes later.

Everything looked fine. Untouched.

But something had happened during those ten minutes.

Most likely, someone had broken in to leave that note.

Jackson turned to me, a concerned tone to his voice as he said, "Whoever did this knew what they were doing. This isn't the work of an amateur. Someone knew to park far enough away that they wouldn't be seen, to disable the cameras at just the right time, and sneak into the house, without being seen or leaving any fingerprints. They knew how to start the video recording again when they were far enough away not to be caught on camera."

My gut tightened.

Someone who worked for the CIA might know how to do that.

But that thought did not bring me any comfort.

As we were talking, Phoebe returned home.

She glanced at us in confusion as she closed the door and hung her purse behind it. "What's going on?"

We filled her in on everything that had happened.

When we finished, she pulled up a chair beside us, and plopped down on it, appearing flabbergasted. "That's so crazy. I've always felt so safe out here."

"This was obviously done by someone who knows what they're doing," Jackson told her.

"So what do we do now?" Phoebe asked. "Should I check my things to see if anything is missing?"

"You can," Jackson told her. "But I doubt your things were touched. This person just wanted to send a message. He or she didn't appear to want to cause us any harm. That's the good news. But the bad news is that they slipped in and out without leaving any clues—except what they wanted to leave."

"Is it safe for you two to stay with me then?" Phoebe asked. "I mean, someone knows you're here."

"If a person is skilled enough to break in without leaving any evidence, then they'll be able to get to us no matter where we are, right?" I couldn't stop myself from asking the question because it wouldn't leave my mind.

Jackson frowned again. "I'm inclined to agree. We can keep moving around, but this person very well could just keep finding us."

I shivered and rubbed my arms again. I'd been

doing that a lot lately. But my chill came from deep inside me.

"So we hunker down here for the evening?" I glanced at Jackson then Phoebe. "Put chairs in front of the doors? Double-check the windows?"

"I'll stay up and make sure that no one gets in," Jackson said.

"But you need to get some sleep also." I worried about him when he did things like that.

Even though he seemed to handle his lack of rest with ease, I knew that couldn't be good on someone's physical or mental state.

"I'm so wired right now that I probably couldn't sleep anyway," Jackson said. "Plus, I want to do some more research, see if there's anything else that I can find out."

It sounded as if Jackson's mind was made up. Instead of arguing, I turned to Phoebe. "Where have you been? If you don't mind me asking."

"A new client up in Kill Devil Hills asked me to dog-sit. He wants me to come over three times a day to let his dog out while he's away from the house working during the day. So I went to meet him and his dog and talk about the details."

"It's going to be a long drive for you," I murmured. "Do you have time?"

"I'll just go before work, on my lunch break, and after work. I think it should be fine."

We talked a few more minutes and then I stood to stretch.

I should probably get some sleep. But my mind still dwelled on that note.

Not everyone is as they seem. At first, I'd assumed that whoever left that note was talking about Adolf or Fake Joey.

But what if it was someone else? Could it be Frank?

I'd only talked to him that one time recently, and that was at the ice cream shop. That theory seemed like a stretch. Besides, why would Frank lie to me?

So who else?

This whole situation just left me more and more disturbed.

CHAPTER
TWENTY-TWO

AFTER I SLIPPED my pajamas on, I sat up in bed, knowing I wasn't ready to sleep either.

As I wondered what I might do with myself, my phone rang.

It was MaryAnn.

Had something happened to her also? What if some drive-by gunman had hit her place? Or if something had happened to Dizzy?

I answered before the first ring had finished sounding.

"Hi, MaryAnn." I tried to keep my voice calm even as my blood raced. "Is everything okay?"

"How could you do this, Joey?"

I stiffened. That *wasn't* what I'd expected her to say. "Do what?"

"You coerced information from my Danny, and now he's been temporarily suspended."

My heart pumped harder. "What?"

"When you ran into us at the restaurant, you were fishing for information. Danny trusted you since you're married to Jackson and since you're my friend. He thought you were telling him the truth."

My heart pounded harder. "MaryAnn . . . I'm so sorry . . . I didn't mean—"

"To you, he might just be an information source. But he's my son. His life matters to me. And it should matter to you also. Everyone's should."

"He does matter—" I started, desperate to explain myself.

"You'll always do whatever it takes to get what you want, no matter who it hurts."

Her words hit me like a slap across the face.

But I wasn't like that. Not anymore. Maybe when I first started in Hollywood, but I'd grown so much.

Hadn't I?

I wanted to believe I'd changed. But what if I'd been fooling myself?

"MaryAnn, I don't know what to say . . ."

"There's nothing you can say." But her voice sounded grim with disappointment.

Before I could even say anything else, I heard a click. She ended the call.

I'd never heard MaryAnn speak to anyone like that. She was the sweetest, nicest person I'd ever met, and she never raised her voice or got angry.

Until now.

A knock sounded, and Jackson stepped inside the bedroom, closing the door behind him. "Everything okay?"

I stared at him. None of this would've ever happened if I hadn't accidentally blurted something about a hit being out on Dizzy.

I stared at him a moment. "Did you report Danny to your superiors?"

He didn't even blink. "I did. I had no other choice."

"Jackson . . . he's on a temporary suspension!"

"We can't have officers sharing classified information with people." His voice sounded grim but not necessarily apologetic.

"It wasn't Danny's fault! It was *mine*. I knew he was an easy target, and I got the information out of him."

"We also can't have officers who are soft targets. That's just a reality of policework."

I crossed my arms, not liking the anger that simmered inside me. "You could've told me, at least."

"I thought about it, but we've had a lot going on today, and it didn't come up yet."

"I just can't believe you did this . . ." I shook my head as I felt a headache coming on.

"I didn't do this to you." Jackson locked his gaze with mine. "I love you, Joey, but you did this to yourself."

I pretended to be sleeping as I listened to Jackson get ready for work the next morning.

I was still upset—even though the person I was primarily upset with was myself.

Still, some of my irritation seemed to spill over onto Jackson. I knew it wasn't right, but I was having trouble reining in those feelings.

After thirty minutes of getting ready, Jackson's hand covered my arm. He leaned over the bed, the fresh scent of his soap floating toward me.

I loved that scent.

He planted a kiss on my cheek. "I hope you have a good day."

So he knew I was awake. Not surprising.

I turned over and stared up at him. "I'll try."

"No hard feelings?"

"That's the goal," I answered honestly.

"I think this will be good for Danny. He has to learn what he can and cannot say."

More heaviness pressed on my chest. I understood, but I wished I hadn't been involved in it. "I just hate that I played a part in his suspension. I should've done better."

"What's done is done. I don't know what else to tell you." Jackson sat on the edge of the bed. "Do you have anything else going on today?"

"I figured you would tell me to hunker down here."

He shrugged. "I thought about it. But whoever got in here to leave that note came and went like a ghost. Plus, I'm not confident that the drive-by shooter is targeting you specifically. And Fake Joey and Fake Dad don't seem to want to cause you any physical harm, at least not yet."

"True." This seems like a weird conversation, but we've had many of these before.

"Besides, even if I told you to stay put, would you?"

"I have that thing at the new museum today," I reminded him. "Are you going to be there?"

"That's right." He snapped his fingers. "How could I have forgotten about opening day?"

"It's like you said last night, we've had a lot going on."

He ran a hand through his hair. "What time are you supposed to be there?"

"Eleven. Which means I probably should get moving now since I need to have breakfast, shower, and travel up north."

"I'll be there. In the meantime, I'll have one of my guys drop off your car. Does that work? I think it's still at the station."

"That would be perfect."

"If you need anything, call me."

"I will."

He watched me another moment before leaning close and giving another tender kiss.

All my bad feelings melted away.

"Is Phoebe still here?" I called behind Jackson as he left.

"No, she left early to do that dog-sitting job. She told me we could help ourselves to whatever is in the fridge."

I tucked that information away.

Then I glanced at the time. It was only 6:30, but Jackson needed to be in early to start his shift.

It would take me an hour to get ready, and I'd need at least an hour to drive up north for the museum opening. But that still left me a couple of hours.

Which was good. Because there was still someone I needed to talk to.

Maybe more than one person.

Wasting no more time, I threw my legs out of bed and started to get ready.

TWENTY-THREE

TWO HOURS LATER, I pulled to a stop in front of Dizzy's house. Her car was still out front, so I hoped to be able to catch her at home.

But I dreaded this conversation.

I knocked at her door, and a moment later she answered wearing a kimono covered in pink flamingos and hot curlers in her hair. Her blue eyeshadow was already in place.

"Joey . . . I wasn't expecting to see you so early."

"I needed to be up for the museum opening. Can I come in?"

She opened the door wider. "Of course."

As I stepped into her house, I felt another rush of nerves.

They were nerves brought about because I knew

I'd done something wrong, and I dreaded fessing up to it.

"Coffee?"

She must have just brewed a pot. The welcoming aroma wafted from the kitchen.

"Thanks, but I think I'm okay." I had actually already had three cups, which was probably a mistake.

"What's wrong, girl?"

"I messed up," I started, my throat unusually dry.

She nodded toward the living room. We went to the couch and sat down before she said, "I know you did."

I sucked in a breath at the lack of surprise in her response. "You do?"

"MaryAnn called last night."

Of *course*! "She's really mad."

"Can you blame her? She feels as if you betrayed her trust and used her and her son."

"That's not what I meant to do." My shoulders slumped.

"Then what did you mean to do?"

I started to answer, but I realized my words would be a direct contradiction of what I just said. I had used Danny's position and temperament in order to find out information.

"It seemed innocent at the time," I finally said. "I had no idea it would lead to this."

Dizzy frowned compassionately. "The truth is, Danny *does* have a big mouth. He shouldn't have told you. But also, you should've been more careful. You were both wrong."

I couldn't argue. I knew that Dizzy's words were honest. In my desperation for answers, I hadn't been very sensible.

"What should I do?" I stared at Dizzy as I waited for her response.

She thought about it a moment before speaking. "I think that MaryAnn will be okay. Just give her a day or so for her emotions to cool down."

"And Danny?"

"Last I heard, he went to Willie Wahoos last night and drank a lot."

"That doesn't sound like Danny."

"Even stranger, apparently he met a girl last night . . . and then he married her."

Danny got drunk and married a stranger.

And this was my fault.

It was all I could think about as I headed toward the museum.

How was I ever going to fix it? That was the question.

And, in the process of trying to fix it, would I only make things worse?

My head pounded, and more than anything I wanted to ditch this ribbon-cutting ceremony right now. But I'd told the museum director I'd be there, and I didn't want to let him down.

I'd already let enough people down.

Still, apprehension bubbled inside me.

I pulled up to the building located on the Currituck Sound in Nags Head. The structure had bright-white wood siding, a black-tin roof, and nautical items that gave the place a maritime vibe.

Inside were artifacts from this region, including shipwreck remnants, items from the Lost Colony, and Native American relics.

Everyone in the area was excited to see the Outer Banks Maritime Museum open.

Not many cars were in the parking lot yet, but I knew that would change in an hour when reporters and other town dignitaries showed up.

I'd been asked to come a little early so I could review the details of the ceremony with everyone involved.

I wiped my hands on the side of my black dress slacks before stepping toward the door, heels clicking across the asphalt. As I walked, I glanced around, and that eerie feeling hit me again.

Was someone watching me? Fake Joey maybe?

And what about Fake Dad? Where was he? Was he okay even?

I had no idea.

And who had left that note at Phoebe's house? I knew it had to be someone skilled and sneaky.

Nothing made sense. I wanted to fix everything for everybody, but I could hardly even fix my own life. How could I manage to help anyone else?

I stepped inside the museum and spotted the curator in the lobby.

That's when I knew I needed to set my other thoughts aside so I could concentrate on this ceremony.

Don Foltz, the curator, greeted me as soon as I walked in. The man reminded me of Albert Einstein with his wide cheeks and crazy white hair. However, his personality was all business and totally Type A.

"Joey . . ." he started. "I'm surprised to see you here so early."

I turned my head. "Why is that? Aren't we still going to talk about the ceremony beforehand?"

He cast me a strange look that made me feel like I was off my rocker or something.

Then he slowly—too slowly, almost as if he

thought I couldn't quickly process things—said, "We already discussed this . . . when you stopped by yesterday."

CHAPTER
TWENTY-FOUR

I STARED AT DON, a sickly feeling in my stomach. "I didn't stop by yesterday."

He chuckled, but the sound quickly faded. "Of course you did. You wore a similar outfit to what you're wearing now, and you said you wanted to see this place a day early. Take some videos. You promised to post about it on your social media to drum up more interest." He squinted and studied me a moment. "Is everything okay?"

I couldn't deny the truth.

Fake Joey had been here.

But why in the world would Fake Joey come to the museum and pretend to be me? It didn't make any sense. She hadn't even posted anything about it on social media. I'd checked this morning for any updates.

For that matter, her page hadn't been taken down yet. I'd been hoping my manager could work his magic, but he hadn't yet.

"Maybe you've heard that there's a woman in the area who's been impersonating me?" I stared at Don as I waited for his response.

"What do you mean?" He looked earnestly confused with that wrinkle between his eyes.

"Someone in this area looks like me and sounds like me and acts like me and is pretending to be me, but this person isn't me. I had no idea she'd show up here. It doesn't make any sense."

He pushed his wire-framed glasses up higher on his nose. "She was very convincing."

"That's what I've heard." I shifted. "I'm really sorry to hear that happened. If I had even thought it was a possibility, I would have called you to warn you. But I didn't think . . ."

He frowned, appearing as if his mind had drifted somewhere else.

I glanced at my watch. I knew we had to run through the ceremony soon. Everyone would be arriving within the next hour.

But I had some more questions first. Then I would call Jackson.

Because if Fake Joey had come here, she'd had a reason, right?

I glanced at Don again. "If you don't mind . . . when you showed this woman around yesterday, was there anything in particular that she seemed interested in?"

"She seemed especially fascinated with this painting of the Bodie Island Lighthouse by master painter Edwin Barrack. She said she had an upcoming role in a top-secret film where she was going to play an art curator and that studying the painting would really help her research the role."

Dread pooled in my stomach. "Any chance I could see this painting?"

"Of course. Come this way."

The curator paused in front of the painting.

I didn't know much about art, but this one was done with acrylics and captured the lighthouse on a stormy day. It really was a beautiful piece, and apparently the artist was world-renowned.

"Did you ever leave her here with this alone?" I asked.

Don thought a moment. "I did get a phone call from someone with a news station. I took the call, but I was probably only gone for five minutes if that. Why?"

I continued to stare at the painting. "Are you sure this is the original painting?"

He chuckled as if my question were absurd. "Of course I'm sure. Why would you ask that?"

"Because something fishy is going on here. How secure is this painting? If someone touches it, will an alarm go off?"

"It will *now*. But yesterday, we were still setting all the alarms up." He paused and gave me another look. "Are you implying what I think you are?"

I didn't bother to try to soften my theory. "I think you should check this painting to make sure it's the real thing."

"There's no way that woman would've gotten out of here with the painting. I would have noticed. All she had was her purse, and that wasn't big enough to fit a painting inside."

"I'm not really sure how she could pull this off. But do you mind humoring me and checking it out anyway?"

He glanced at his watch, not hiding his crankiness at my suggestion. "We don't have much time."

"In that case, I'd suggest looking now."

CHAPTER
TWENTY-FIVE

"IT'S A FAKE!" Curator Don ran a hand through his hair. "I can't believe this. How did you know?"

I frowned, somehow feeling like this was my fault.

I clearly had baggage in my life because I felt as if everything was my fault. I mean, don't get me wrong, there were plenty of things that *were* my fault. Like Officer Danny. And that time I threw up at a crime scene and contaminated it.

But this one, I truly had nothing to do with.

I'd already called Jackson, and he was on his way here.

A few minutes later, when he stepped into the room in his jeans and washed-out blue T-shirt, I gave him the update. The curator interjected his thoughts as he paced frantically in circles around us.

"Do you have any video cameras set up yet?" Jackson asked.

The curator shook his head. "Not yet. We are wrapping up all those final touches. I mean, there are security cameras outside. But we didn't think anyone would get through *that* security to come in here and do anything. I never thought it could be someone from within." He scowled at me as if I was the one who'd switched out the paintings.

"I had nothing to do with this," I reminded him. "It was the other me."

He ran a hand through his hair again, leaving it standing on end—very Albert Einstein-ish. "I know. I know!"

"This woman just took this to the next level," Jackson said. "Not only is she impersonating you, but now she's committing theft."

"Do you think that's what this was all about?" I asked him. "She impersonated me all this time because she knew I'd be at the ceremony and that would give her the opportunity to steal the lighthouse painting?"

"I don't know." Jackson took out his phone. "It's definitely a theory worth looking into."

As Jackson stepped away to inform his colleagues of what was going on, I looked back at Don. "Are we still going to do the ribbon-cutting ceremony?"

His eyes narrowed again as his Type A personality seemed to be on the verge of unraveling.

"No," he practically snapped as he threw his hands in the air. "Everything is ruined now, and in less than an hour, everyone in the Outer Banks is going to know about it!"

Jackson agreed that the ribbon-cutting ceremony should be postponed.

The police would need time to investigate, which meant they'd need to limit the number of people coming inside the museum. Apparently, the FBI would need to be called in also because they handled art crimes.

Who knew one little painting could cause such a stir?

Finally, after I'd been at the museum two hours, I was free to go.

I couldn't wait to have some time to think through what had happened.

But as soon as I stepped outside, I spotted Amanda near a news van talking to the same cameraman from yesterday.

I quickly slipped behind the corner before she spotted me.

Don had said a reporter called him, which had been the opening Fake Joey had needed to steal that painting.

What if that reporter was Amanda?

I could hardly breathe as the theory swished around in my mind.

Wasting no time, I rushed back inside and found Don. I had to ask him about that phone call.

He looked super irritated as I approached him—almost as if he still believed I was responsible for this whole fiasco.

"I know you're busy," I started. "But you mentioned that a reporter called you and that's what distracted you while the person impersonating me was here?"

"That's right." His scowl deepened.

"This reporter . . . was it a man or a woman?" I thought I already knew that answer, I needed confirmation.

"A man," he said as he turned his nose up.

My eyebrows flung up in surprise. "Really?"

"Yes, really," he answered tersely. "Anything else I can help you with, Mrs. Darling?"

My public name was still Darling, even though legally I'd changed it to Joey Sullivan.

I could tell this man was *not* in the mood to answer any more questions, so I excused myself.

Jackson was just wrapping up a conversation with another detective in the lobby when I walked up. I told him about the discussion I'd just had with the curator.

He let out all the appropriate grunts and nods as he listened, hand on his chin. "This is all very strange. Of all the turns and twists I saw coming with this Fake Joey, this wasn't one of them."

For real. Me either.

I shook my head. "Any updates on Fake Dad?"

"Not yet. We have people out there looking for him, but as of yet we haven't found him."

I drew in a deep breath before diving into the next subject. "There's one more thing I thought I should mention to you. I talked to Dizzy this morning, and she told me that . . ."

"What is it, Joey?" Jackson studied my face.

I swallowed hard as the words lodged in my throat. "It's about Danny."

"Go on."

"Apparently, he . . . well, he got married last night."

Jackson's lips parted and his pitch climbed as he said, "What?"

I nodded. "I couldn't believe it either."

He ran a hand over his face and looked off into

the distance before turning to me again. "I'll talk to him and see what's going on."

I nodded. "That sounds like a good idea."

I would volunteer to join him, but I feared my help was the last thing Danny would want.

CHAPTER
TWENTY-SIX

SINCE I WAS free to leave the museum, I thought it was probably best if I did just that.

I glanced out the front window first and saw that Amanda and her cameraman were now gone.

Relief washed through me.

As I walked to my car, I couldn't help but think about how Fake Joey might have gotten that painting out of the building. It would have been too big to slip into her purse, and she couldn't have risked folding it. That would be foolish.

Would she have had time in the five minutes that the curator was gone to switch out the painting and then stash it somewhere to retrieve later?

There was an emergency exit door in the adjoining room where the painting had been displayed.

What were the chances Fake Joey had slipped the real painting outside and come back later to pick it up? In fact, she would have had to leave a forged painting out there also to swap out.

Don had said they had cameras set up on the outside of the building. Had one of those picked up on something? Or had they been like the security camera at Phoebe's house and mysteriously gone black for ten minutes?

I didn't want to be a pessimist, but that seemed like the most likely scenario. I was sure Jackson and his colleagues would look into it. To be extra sure, next time I talked to Jackson, I would run the idea past him.

I reached my car, but instead of getting inside, I took a detour toward the back of the building.

My curiosity couldn't be stopped. It was a curse. Or a blessing.

Really, it was hard to say and depended on the day.

No one else was back here, which surprised me. But I paused beside that emergency exit and stared at it a minute.

If Fake Joey had been working quickly, she could have definitely slipped open that door and stashed it outside. Ordinarily, an alarm would probably go off when the door was opened. But that system may not have been set up yesterday.

I knew museum staff were running behind schedule and rushing to get things done in time. Fake Joey could have used that to her advantage.

As I glanced at the ground, I spotted something on the sand near the door.

A footprint. A man-sized footprint.

I pulled out my phone and took a picture—but only after placing one of my credit cards there for size. I'd learned that trick from Raven.

Then, as I climbed in my car, I texted the photo to Jackson with a note that maybe he should check it out.

Would this redeem me from all of my snafus?

No way.

But maybe it was a start.

I left the museum, but I honestly didn't know what to do with myself. I didn't want to return to Phoebe's. What would I do there? Stare at the wall?

No thank you.

I supposed I could grab some lunch. It was two o'clock already.

Or I could try to talk to MaryAnn . . . but Dizzy

had said to give her a day, so that wasn't a great idea either.

While I sat at a red light, Dizzy texted me. My car read it aloud.

> She's at it again.

The next moment, a link appeared on my screen.

I pulled off into a parking lot and threw my car into Park.

My finger trembled slightly before I clicked on the link. I had a feeling I knew what this was.

More media from Fake Joey.

I was right.

Another live video appeared.

And it showed Fake Joey outside my favorite hangout—Sunrise Coffee.

Something close to anger boiled up inside me.

It was time to get some answers. No more Mrs. Nice Girl.

I was confronting this lady head-on.

CHAPTER
TWENTY-SEVEN

AS SOON AS I spotted Sunrise Coffee in the distance, I noticed the crowd outside.

Wasn't that just peachy?

Apparently, Fake Joey's last video where she'd encouraged fans to track her down had worked.

Just how long had this woman been filming today for people to know about her location and have time to get here?

I supposed that didn't really matter.

I parked in the lot the next building over and then crossed the street.

Fake Joey was doing selfies with my fans as I walked up.

I pushed through the crowd amidst gasps around me. People began to murmur, but I kept going until I paused in front of Fake Joey.

She finished taking her selfie with the fan beside her, and her smile disappeared as she lowered the camera.

"What do you think you're doing?" I demanded as I tapped into my inner Raven.

"I figured you'd show up eventually." Fake Joey turned to the crowd around us. "Everyone, this is the woman who's been impersonating me."

My mouth dropped open. "*She's* the fake Joey."

"No, don't listen to her. She's just trying to make my life miserable."

My mouth opened farther.

I couldn't believe she was doing this. But she was.

I stared at my doppelganger, amazed at how much she looked like me.

But I noted that her eyes were a lighter shade of brown, even though the shape was pretty close. Hearing her in person, I also noted her voice didn't sound exactly like mine.

As the wind blew her hair from her face, another detail caught my eye. A line of dry skin stretched near her hairline.

But was that really dry skin? Or was this woman wearing some type of prosthetic? Just like they did in the spy movies? Was this woman going all *Mission Impossible*?

Would Tom Cruise appear next and start jumping on a couch?

I didn't know. But a part of me wanted to rip off her face to reveal the real woman beneath the façade.

I supposed that would just land me in deeper water, however. Especially if I was wrong and that was her real face.

Instead, I stared at her. "I don't know what you're trying to get from this, but you need to stop."

"You're the one who needs to stop." Fake Joey turned to the crowd around us again, clearly knowing how to work them. "Everyone, we need to let it be known that it's not okay to impersonate someone else. Am I right?"

The crowd began to both cheer and boo—cheering at her words and booing at me.

I'd never been so heckled.

Two could play this game.

I turned to the crowd also. "You have got this all wrong. I'm the real Joey Darling, and this woman is pretending to be me. Don't listen to anything she says."

"The real Joey loves us!" a woman in the crowd yelled. "The real Joey doesn't mind doing selfies."

"I don't mind doing selfies with people." I tried to keep the outrage from my voice.

What had I ever done in all my years in showbiz

to make my fans think I didn't like them? I was usually known for being too nice!

The woman's statement didn't make any sense.

My irritation grew stronger by the moment. How could this look-alike be winning right now? It didn't seem possible.

"Everyone, I've got to get out of here." Fake Joey held up her hands as if to part the crowd. "Please make sure she doesn't follow me."

I scoffed.

The nerve of that woman . . .

She shoved past me, leaning close enough to whisper, "Watch your back."

Then the crowd closed around me as she made her getaway.

I wasn't sure the angry mob around me would let me go.

I also knew it would do no good for me to explain that I truly was the real Joey Darling. Their minds were already made up.

Instead, I pushed past the people surrounding me and went into the coffee shop.

Thankfully, none of them followed.

Shannon, the barista, glanced at me from behind the counter before smiling cautiously.

I waved at her as I headed toward the back of the building. I made sure to rub Java's—the resident golden doodle—ears quicky as I went by.

Then I opened the back exit, careful not to let out the tabby cat that also called this place home.

I'd seen Fake Joey head in this direction.

Sure enough, she'd parked behind the building.

I watched as she climbed into a red sports car with a man.

My breath caught.

He was the same man I'd spotted her with behind the grocery store.

Right now, the window was down, and his arm rested casually on the door.

My breath caught again.

Some type of red splatter stained his sleeve.

Blood?

Was this man a killer?

My head began to spin.

"Is everything okay?"

I flinched and turned to see Shannon behind me.

The twentysomething woman was a ceramist who'd made many of the mugs sold here in the shop. Working as a barista helped her make ends meet.

But right now, she looked . . . unsettled.

I couldn't blame her for being on edge, not after that scene outside.

"I'm sorry . . . I know this is weird. And I know you probably think I'm impersonating Joey Darling."

"No, I know you're the real Joey Darling."

I stared at her, unsure if I had heard her correctly. "How can you tell?"

"Your highlights. They're different than hers."

I touched my hair. "What?"

She nodded. "Hers are thicker than yours and farther apart. I know it seems like a weird thing to notice, but it's something I observed."

Satisfaction filled me.

There were advantages to being around artists who had an eye for detail.

I grinned. "You're a lifesaver, Shannon."

"Thank you?" It almost sounded like a question.

Now at least I had something to work with.

But before I did any snooping out back, I would grab some coffee and then wait for the crowd outside to clear. They were already thinning out.

Now I just needed to give it a few minutes.

I SAT in the corner of the coffee shop, facing the door so I could see who came inside.

Jackson called as I sipped my coffee.

"The FBI wants to talk to you," he announced.

My back stiffened at his words, and I placed my mug back on the table. "What?"

"You're part of the art investigation. It was only a matter of time."

"But what if they think I'm guilty?" Panic raced inside me.

"That won't happen . . . probably."

My mouth dropped open. "Probably?"

Not. Comforting.

"I mean, it won't happen," Jackson corrected. "This is just standard procedure."

I leaned back in my chair and tried to get my racing thoughts under control. "When?"

"I'm not sure yet. I'll let you know. I'll make sure to be the one who brings you in."

"Thanks . . . I guess." Fake Joey really wanted to make my life miserable.

She was succeeding.

He paused a moment before saying, "I just saw your confrontation on social media."

I frowned at the memory. "I'm here at the coffee house now."

"I'm not sure confronting this woman was a good idea."

"She turned things back on me, so it didn't matter. She had the upper hand the whole time . . . and I don't like it."

"Rightfully so."

"The same man I saw her meeting with at the grocery store was here. *And* I saw something dry at the edge of her face around her hairline. Is she in need of a facial? I don't think so. She was wearing some type of prosthetic."

"Good observation."

"And a sharp-eyed barista who works here noticed that Fake Joey's highlights are slightly different than mine."

"What highlights? Video highlights?"

"No, silly. Hair highlights." I almost rolled my eyes, but I didn't.

"Oh . . . of course. At least, that's something to go on."

I released a breath. "Something is better than nothing."

Why did I keep saying that? I supposed because it was true.

"Do you want me to pick you up?" he asked.

I took another sip of my coffee as I considered his question. Finally, I said, "No, I'm fine."

"If you change your mind, let me know."

"I will. Have you talked to Danny?"

"He's not answering his phone, and he's not at home."

I was about to take another sip of my coffee, but I lowered the cup back to the table and frowned. A bad feeling churned in my stomach.

Was Danny okay? What if what I'd done had led him down a bad path?

How would I ever forgive myself?

Coffee wasn't much of a lunch. Now I was jittery on top of already being anxious.

I still didn't have a clear plan of where to go

today.

So I did the next best thing.

I headed to Oh Buoy, the smoothie bar where Phoebe worked.

I needed to get something solid in my stomach, and this place had fabulous wraps and fruity drinks.

I slipped inside, thankful to see that Fake Joey hadn't beat me here. Then I sat on a barstool in front of Phoebe and placed my order—a Coquina Crush smoothie, a chicken Caesar wrap, a chocolate chip cookie, and a bag of chips, with an apple on the side.

Phoebe gave me a look after I finished rattling off what I wanted. "You sure you don't want to start with the smoothie and wrap?"

Her words hit me, snapping me out of my binging stupor. "Yes, of course. Sorry—my stomach and anxiety took over my lips."

"I take it today isn't going well." Phoebe glanced at me before adding some strawberries to a metal cup. In the background, the buzz of blenders filled the air, drowning out the chatter around me.

This restaurant wasn't necessarily the best place to talk because of that, but the food was delicious and healthy.

"No, things are not going well at all."

She added more fruit to the cup. "Everyone in

here has been talking about how the museum didn't open on time."

I tried to mask my disgust. "I didn't know people were that excited about it."

"I'm not sure if people were truly excited about it, but locals have a lot of theories about what might have happened to that painting." She glanced around. "Can you talk about it?"

I thought about her question before remembering Danny. I didn't want to be Loose Lips Joey.

"It's probably better if I don't right now," I finally said. "But as soon as I can, I will. What I can tell you is . . ."

I gave her an update on the situation with Fake Joey this morning.

"I just can't imagine what this girl's endgame might be." Phoebe paused long enough to shake her head.

"That's exactly what I need to figure out. This isn't somebody who is innocently impersonating me. She wants something. She has a very conniving side. That was clear after what happened today when she whispered that I needed to watch my back."

She added some protein powder to the cup. "I don't like where this is going."

I frowned. "Me either."

"Give me a sec." Phoebe stuck her cup into the blender, and a grinding sound filled the air again.

As she poured the drink into a tall paper cup and topped it with a lid and straw, I continued, "Enough about me. How's it going with the new client? You checked on his dog this morning?"

"Pete is amazing."

"Pete?"

"He's the husky. And apparently his owner is a photographer or something. He has all this equipment—cameras and things."

"Interesting."

Before we could talk anymore, my phone buzzed. I glanced at the screen and saw it was a text from Fake Dad.

My breath caught. Was he okay?

I quickly clicked on it.

There were only two words in the message.

Help me.

CHAPTER
TWENTY-NINE

AS I STARED at the text, I remembered the note left in Phoebe's house. The note warning me that not everyone was as they seemed.

Fake Dad definitely didn't seem safe or trustworthy. However, he had been abducted. I'd seen it with my own eyes.

"What are you going to do?" Phoebe stared at my phone.

My fingers poised over the keyboard as I considered my options.

"I'm going to respond," I decided. "I'm not going to promise anything. I'm going to see if I can get some more information about the situation."

I typed:

What happened?

I was abducted. They say they'll kill me if you don't meet them.

I swallowed hard.

Where?

I can send location, but not now.

Phoebe leaned closer and shook her head. "Don't do it, Joey."

"I'm not going to do anything irrational. Like I said, I'm just getting more information."

I glanced back at the screen, wondering if I only had a short window to respond. If Fake Dad had been abducted, then no doubt the people who took him were reading this. There could be a time limit. Someone could even be watching me right now.

At the thought, I glanced around.

I didn't see anyone's eyes on me.

"Joey . . . what kind of dad would ask you to do this?" Phoebe stared at me, her work seemingly forgotten. "Would ask you to put yourself in danger."

"Good point," I muttered.

When I was silent a few seconds, Fake Dad texted again.

They want you to come this evening at eight. I'm sorry, Joey.

I stared at those words.

I hated being in this position.

If he really was tricking me, which I had a feeling he was, this could all be a setup.

But if by chance there was any truth to this, his life could be in my hands.

Jackson strode inside Oh Buoy as I was picking at my wrap. My appetite seemed to disappear yet again.

"You following me?" I asked as he paused beside me at the bar.

"I happened to be driving by and saw your car outside. I decided I should check on you . . . and I knew seeing your beautiful face could cheer me up."

My heart felt a little gooey at his words, and I nearly forgot about all my problems.

"Do you want your normal?" Phoebe asked Jackson.

He nodded.

She quickly threw a strawberry banana smoothie together for him, and the blender whirled again as she mixed it.

After paying, we went out to Jackson's SUV for some privacy.

This didn't seem like the kind of conversation that we should have in public.

I climbed into the front seat beside him.

"Are you sure you're doing okay?" He studied my face the way he always did—with genuine interest and concern.

I filled him in on the texts Fake Dad had sent and then showed him the messages.

His muscles tightened. "You know you can't meet him, right?"

I released a sigh. "I know. But I'm still struggling with . . . everything, I suppose."

"I have an update for you as well." Jackson shifted toward me, his expression still serious.

"You do?" I sat up straighter.

"We got a fingerprint match back on Adolf."

"Where did you get his fingerprint?"

"I grabbed his fork after we ate with him at The Egg Bistro." Jackson didn't say "of course," but it was implied.

Admiration rushed through me. "Have I told you you're brilliant?"

"I *have* learned a few things in my years as a detective."

"Yes, you have. Now, enough flattering you. Who

is this guy? You have a name?"

"His first name *is* Adolf. Although his friends call him Doughy, which I can only assume is short for Dolf. Last name is Casperson."

"So he gave me his real first name. I guess that's a good thing." Uncertainty weakened my statement.

"By all appearances, he really is CIA."

"Really?" Did that mean he was respectable?

Was the CIA respectable? I wanted to say they were, but I didn't know for sure.

"He went off the grid, and none of his colleagues have talked to him in the past three months."

That was interesting . . .

But I had a more pressing question. "Is he my father?"

Silence stretched as I waited for his answer. It seemed like hours passed when it was really mere seconds.

But so much hinged on Jackson's answer.

Maybe if Adolf *was* my father, I really didn't want to know.

Or did I?

Jackson squeezed my hand. "We don't know yet, but we're looking into it."

I frowned.

It couldn't be quite as simple as a yes or no, could it?

CHAPTER
THIRTY

I TOOK another sip of my smoothie as I sat in Jackson's SUV mulling over our conversation. My thoughts were racing in so many different directions.

Finally, I cleared my throat as I brought up what I knew would be a touchy subject.

"What do you think about contacting Ted Manson?" I asked.

Jackson looked at me and blinked. "Special Agent Manson? Why would we do that?"

"Because he's the only one who might know where my father—my *real* father—is and if he's okay."

"They would've told you if he wasn't okay, Joey."

"Really?" No one had explained that to me when I said goodbye to my father.

"Really. If he wasn't okay, then there would be no reason for him to be hidden anymore." Jackson squeezed my hand again.

I knew what he was saying. That if my father was dead, authorities would tell me. But what if he wasn't dead, but just in danger? Or missing?

"The thing is," Jackson said, "it's not a good idea to contact him. It could put your father at greater risk. I know that's hard to hear. You've been a real trouper about this."

"But he might have some of the answers I need." I tried not to pout, but I felt pouty.

"But what's more important? Having answers or keeping him alive?"

I frowned again.

I didn't even have to answer that question. It was obvious. Clearly, my dad's life was more important.

I glanced at my phone.

That text had said to meet at eight o'clock tonight and that Fake Dad would send me the location.

How could I wait until then? What would I do when he did send me that location?

"Maybe we could do a sting," I muttered.

"What?"

I realized I needed to explain myself better. "Tonight. When I get the location from Fake Dad.

Maybe we can set up some officers and . . . I don't know. Take the bad guys down. Get some answers."

"Maybe."

At least Jackson didn't outright say no.

I took that as a good sign.

"How about those people that did the drive-by shootings? Were they really Russian? Can you tell me that at least?" I didn't want to press my luck by asking too many questions and getting Jackson suspended as well.

Jackson had a little more common sense than Danny. Actually, *a lot* more common sense.

He nodded. "It appears they are."

CIA? Russia? Drive-by shootings? This had the makings of a good spy thriller.

Could all of this be about that missing painting? I knew the piece was worth a lot of money, but it just didn't seem to fit everything else that was happening.

Before I could think about it much longer, I spotted someone walking into Oh Buoy.

It was Danny . . . with a woman I'd never seen before.

The two held hands.

The rumor was true, wasn't it?

Danny *had* gotten married.

Jackson quickly opened his SUV door and rushed out. "Danny!"

Danny paused and turned back to Jackson.

The man looked out of it. Hungover, if I had to guess.

I scrambled out behind Jackson and paused beside him as I stared at Danny.

As Danny's gaze slid over to me, his brow furrowed.

"You . . ." he growled.

"I know you're mad at me," I rushed. "I'm so, so sorry."

Really, he looked horrible. *So* horrible.

More guilt pounded at me.

If I hadn't asked those questions, Danny wouldn't be in this situation right now.

My gaze shifted to the pretty woman beside him. She was a thin brunette with puckered lips and a sharp gaze.

"Who is this?" Jackson kept his voice polite.

If I had to guess, it was taking all of his willpower to remain on his best behavior right now.

Danny gripped the woman's hand tighter. "This is my wife, Sasha."

Sasha? Just because the name sounded Russian didn't mean that she was . . . right?

Her lips puckered further as if she were a model known for her stuck-up expressions. "Nice to meet you."

My blood froze.

The woman *definitely* had a Russian accent.

Danny had met someone at a bar last night and spontaneously gotten married. The woman was Russian. *And* there were Russians in this area who were possibly involved in an abduction and drive-by shootings.

My head was spinning.

What had Danny been thinking?

Some of my guilt over his suspension disappeared.

I hated to say it, but maybe he *shouldn't* be a police officer.

"Look, Danny . . ." Jackson glanced at Sasha then back at Danny again. "Can we talk privately?"

Danny's new wife nodded toward the door. "I'll just go inside and order for us."

"You know what I like, right?" Danny's gaze lingered on her.

How in the world would that woman know what he liked? She didn't even know him.

But she nodded and smiled. "Mirlo Sunrise?"

Danny practically glowed at her. "That's the one."

Sasha flashed him another sultry grin as she opened the door. "That sounds great."

Then she disappeared inside.

I WASN'T sure if I would be shooed away by Danny now that Sasha was gone. I knew that Danny didn't like me very much, and he'd been being polite.

But he didn't ask me to leave. Not yet.

Jackson stepped closer to his colleague, his expression a mix of concern and irritation. "Danny . . . what were you thinking? Didn't you just meet this woman? We're all worried about you."

Danny's gaze darkened. "If you were that worried about me, maybe you shouldn't have suspended me."

Jackson's jaw tightened. "The suspension is temporary while we review a few things. We went over that with you yesterday."

Danny didn't seem to care about Jackson's reassurance. He stared off into the distance with a cold, hard look in his bloodshot eyes.

"Who is this woman that you married?" Jackson asked.

"We met last night and hit it off. She's wonderful. Won . . . der . . . ful." Danny emphasized each syllable as if to drive home his point—but his haggard gaze made it hard to take him seriously.

"Danny . . ." My voice trailed as I tried to figure out how to tell him his new wife might be conning him.

His shoulders slumped. "Look, I know I'm a loser—"

"You're not a loser, Danny." I squeezed his arm as compassion filled me. "I should've never asked you for that information."

"I don't really share classified information often." He hung his head as if in shame. "I don't."

"Once is one time too many." Jackson scowled at him before continuing with his questions. "Who even married you at such a late hour?"

"One of my buddies from high school was ordained online last week." He shrugged. "He married us."

Online ordination?

Maybe there was a chance the marriage wasn't legit.

That was the only comfort I could find in this situation.

Jackson ran a hand over his face as he often did when frustrated.

This conversation with Danny was exasperating.

Danny obviously had too much to drink last night and made some poor decisions. It didn't help that he was known for making poor decisions, even when alcohol wasn't involved.

"You didn't go home last night," Jackson continued. "Where did you go for your wedding night?"

Danny scowled again. "I'd rather not say."

Something about his inflection made me super curious.

There was a story there. I was certain of it.

"Danny . . ." Jackson's voice held a warning.

Danny let out a breath as if already caving from the soft interrogation Jackson was giving him.

"Fine." Danny crossed his arms. "We went to . . . your place. Sasha wanted to see where Joey lives."

"What?" My response popped out quick and high-pitched. Certainly, I hadn't heard him correctly.

"Sasha is a big fan. She—"

"I've seen big fans before," I told him. "She didn't seem impressed."

"She's just shy. And . . . I'm mad at you." Danny gave me a pointed look. "I knew you weren't staying there so I figured, what would it hurt? Maybe I could impress my new wife. Because as soon as she gets to know me, she certainly won't be impressed."

I really wanted to give him a good pep talk right here, but there were other issues at hand that I needed to address first—like Danny breaking into my house.

But Jackson beat me to it. "Danny . . . did you leave Sasha alone at our house at any point?"

"I mean . . ." He shrugged. "I eventually fell asleep. She wasn't really alone. I don't think . . ."

I didn't even try to repress my scowl.

Jackson let out a long breath as if he needed a moment to compose himself.

"I need to talk to Sasha." Jackson stormed toward the smoothie shop and stepped inside.

But he emerged only seconds later, and his dirty look had only deepened.

Jackson glanced at me and then Danny before announcing, "She's gone. Sasha went in the front door and slipped out the back."

I NEVER THOUGHT I'd feel so weird stepping into my own place. But I did.

However, I missed my home. I loved this place. I loved looking out the windows and seeing the ocean in the morning. I loved listening to the birds outside and the tourists filled with joy as they frolicked in the ocean.

I loved the life that Jackson and I had started together here.

Now I needed to sanitize this whole house.

Not just because Danny and his wife had their wedding night here without my permission.

But because I felt like this Sasha woman was connected to the mayhem in my life, and I had no idea what she'd been doing here. My house had been violated.

How had Danny even gotten into the place?

Then I remembered we'd had him housesit while we were on our honeymoon. He must have made a copy of the key—probably out of fear he'd lose one.

I could definitely see that happening.

Jackson and I paused in our living room and glanced around. My gaze stopped on the plywood covering my front window, and I frowned. That was just one more reminder of everything that happened.

"I know the quickest thing to do would be to split up to see if we notice anything different," Jackson said. "But I think we should stick together."

I was thankful he'd said that because my brain didn't feel like it was working correctly. I didn't want to take a chance and miss anything.

We went room by room and looked for anything that might be out of place.

But we didn't see anything.

Except for a couple of used bath towels left on the bathroom floor and rumpled bed sheets in the spare bedroom.

Gross. I might just have to burn them and buy a new set.

At least, at first glance, it didn't look like anything had been stolen.

However, the woman may not have wanted to steal anything of value. Not financial value at least.

Did I have anything here that someone from the CIA or Russia would want?

That's when an idea hit me.

"What are you thinking, Joey?" Jackson asked as he followed behind me to the third floor.

I continued to one of the guest bedrooms.

When I moved in here, I hadn't felt like organizing things.

So there were several items I'd simply tucked away in closets and under beds.

I didn't think Jackson had seen the spare rooms since I moved all my things here. He hadn't had a reason to.

I'd successfully hidden my junk from him for the past two months. But now he was going to find out the truth about exactly what a hot mess I was.

I opened a spare bedroom closet and glanced at all the boxes piled haphazardly against the wall inside.

"What is all of this stuff?" Jackson sounded like he'd just stepped into an episode of *Hoarders*.

"I'm going to get around to organizing it." I shrugged.

"When?" He gave me another look.

"When I'm on a break from filming."

"Do you mean like, now?" He dropped his head to the side as he stared at me.

"Well, I would. But I can't because . . . you know Fake Joey, Fake Dad . . ." I began ticking off the reasons on my fingers before shuffling through some boxes.

"Can I help?" Jackson stepped back and crossed his arms, looking like the last thing he wanted was to delve into my random belongings.

"No, I've got this. I know exactly where it is."

Organized chaos. Wasn't that what people called such things?

My office also contained my own special filing system—one that consisted of piles of papers all over the top of my desk.

Finally, on the top shelf of the closet, I found the metal box I was looking for.

I carried it to the bed and sat down, staring at it a moment as memories hit me.

Jackson lowered himself on the other side of the box. "What's this?"

"Remember when I first moved here, and I was looking for my dad when he'd gone missing that first time?"

He nodded.

"When I discovered that storage facility where he

had rented a space, this was in the old wooden trunk inside. Remember? There was also an American flag, my dad's old Bible, my grandma's handmade quilt, and that bull statue that I love."

"That's right. I remember that. What do you think is inside this box that someone might have been looking for?"

I drew in a deep breath and then released it. Instead of answering, I opened the box.

I stared at the contents. There were birth certificates, social security cards, and insurance information.

I shuffled through them and found all the things that were supposed to be there.

Except one.

"Joey?" Jackson still stared at me, obviously not knowing what I had been looking for.

"That Sasha woman . . . she stole my birth certificate."

"WHY WOULD someone want your birth certificate?" Jackson asked as he began to pace the spare bedroom.

"I don't know. This whole situation is just weird."

"You can say that again." He stared off in the distance. "Does this Adolf guy need your certificate to prove you're related?"

"I'm not sure. I'd think a DNA test would be the best way to prove it."

"Maybe, but that takes time. Perhaps more time than he wants to wait."

"It's hard to say. Honestly, I'm fresh out of ideas."

Jackson's phone rang, and he stepped into the hallway to answer. He reappeared a moment later, and I knew he had another update.

"Bronxy wants to talk," he announced.

"Bronxy?" I was clearly missing something.

"He's the guy someone tried to hire to be a hitman. Remember?"

"That's right." Danny had mentioned him. I fought a frown at the memory. "He wants to talk?"

"We let him out so he could meet with a guy who could've potentially been hired for that same job."

"Did he discover anything?"

"That's what I'm about to find out. He only wants to talk to me."

"So what do I do in the meantime?"

Jackson started toward the door. "You're going to come with me."

I felt like a girl who had just been handed exactly what she wanted for Christmas. "Really?"

Jackson nodded. "Really. Let's go."

I stared at Bronxy as he sat at the interrogation table. The man didn't look as I had assumed he would.

I guess I imagined he'd be a thug-like guy with scars, broken teeth, and massive tattoos.

But he looked surprisingly normal. Probably five foot nine with a buzz of light brown hair, a thin nose, and wide cheeks. He wore black jeans and a white T-shirt.

If I'd run into him on the street, I probably wouldn't have an inkling that he was dangerous.

Maybe that's what made him so good at his job.

"Joey Darling," he started. "I can't tell you what a big fan I am."

"Thanks." I tucked my chair up under the table, not exactly sure how to respond to his comment in this situation.

Thankfully, we didn't have much time for chitchat because Jackson jumped right in, leaning on the table as he stared the man down. "What did you find out?"

He shifted slowly, moving each leg as if they were laden with weights. "Turns out, my friend was approached by someone about this job."

My heart quickened as I listened.

"And what did he say?" Jackson asked.

"He got a little bit further into the process than I did. He talked to these guys on the phone, so there's no way he would be able to identify them. But he did say they had a slight accent."

Russian. But I didn't say that aloud.

"Anything else that could be of value and give us incentive to cut you a deal?" Jackson asked.

"Unlike me, they texted him a picture of this target. My friend showed it to me."

Now, my heart really pounded harder.

Who was it? Because it really seemed as if the

shootings were random, and no one was really being targeted.

"Wish I could've taken a picture of the picture, but I didn't have a cell phone, thanks to you." Bronxy gave Jackson a dirty look. "But the guy in the photo . . . he was tall with dark hair and a thin build."

He didn't have to go any farther. I knew exactly where this was going.

Jackson pulled a picture from his pocket and slid it across the table.

It was a picture of Fake Dad. The photo looked as if it had been taken from a security camera in the breakfast joint when we met.

Jackson had all kinds of things up his sleeve during that meeting, hadn't he? Things he hadn't mentioned to me.

"Yes." Bronxy jabbed his finger at the picture. "That was him. These guys offered to pay a hundred thousand to shoot him and make it look random."

"Why did you say no?"

"I've done a lot of bad things in my life, but I don't want to add murder to that list."

"But . . . I thought you were a hitman," I muttered.

He stared at me in confusion a moment. "Why would you think that?"

"Aren't you?" I asked.

"No! Sure, I take little jobs here and there. Maybe a robbery or a con job. I've even roughed people up. But murder? No way."

"How did these guys find your name then?" I was still trying to make sense of this.

"In the crime world, you might be surprised by the connections you make—especially with your old cellmates."

"Noted." I nodded.

Jackson jumped in with his interrogation. "Why didn't your friend take the job?"

"They told him to think about it. Before he made up his mind, they called again and said they decided to do the job themselves."

CHAPTER
THIRTY-FOUR

AFTER TALKING TO BRONXY, the FBI questioned me—thoroughly, I might add. By the time they finished, it was getting dark.

I noticed I'd missed a couple of calls from Phoebe, and I tried to call her back, but she didn't answer. She was probably checking on that dog she took care of after work.

I glanced at my watch. I was supposed to get instructions any time now if I wanted to meet Fake Dad and try to get him released.

Which I knew Jackson would never go for. I appreciated that he was protective of me like that. But I knew I'd live with guilt if something happened to Adolf.

Officer Shiver, a new recruit working the front desk, wandered toward us, a bewildered expression on her face. "Detective Sullivan, I went to the bathroom for a few minutes. When I came back this was on my desk."

She placed an envelope on the desk in front of Jackson.

I stared at it and saw my name scrawled on it.

"You didn't see who left it?" Jackson asked as he studied the envelope.

"I didn't," she said. "But I'll check the security footage."

"You do that. I'd like an image of the person who brought this in."

"Got it." Officer Shiver walked back toward the desk.

Jackson and I both looked down at the envelope. Then he pulled some gloves from his drawer and carefully opened the letter.

A picture was inside.

He slid it onto his desk so we could both see.

Based on the coloring, it was an older photo.

On it was a girl, probably five or six, holding an old, raggedy bunny and standing beside a man.

"Does this look familiar to you?" Jackson asked.

My head spun. "That's me. And that's Bunny-Boo, the stuffed animal I carried around until I was seven. That man beside me? That's my Fake Dad when he was younger. But I don't remember this picture being taken."

Eight o'clock came and went, and there were no texts from Fake Dad.

I even texted him.

But no one responded.

The whole thing made me feel helpless.

As I picked at a salad someone had brought me, I couldn't get that picture out of my mind. The one of me. With Bunny-Boo. With Fake Dad.

It almost seemed to confirm that this man *could* be my father.

Jackson had given the photo to one of his CSI guys to examine it and see if it had been photo-shopped.

In the meantime, Officer Shiver had gotten the images from the security camera outside the police station showing the person who dropped this off.

But it was impossible to tell anything about the figure, who'd been clad in a black hat and jacket. Could it have been Sasha? Or the man Fake Joey had met with?

Maybe.

"What now?" I glanced up at Jackson as he typed

away on his computer while grabbing a fry from the hinged paper container in front of him.

"Right now, I feel like you should just get back to Phoebe's. I don't know what's going on, but we're not going to figure out anything tonight. I have officers on standby, but if this guy doesn't text us, our hands are tied."

I frowned but stood. I'd figured that's what he would say. "What about you?"

"I'll follow behind you."

Five minutes later, we were both on the road. Leaving Nags Head, Jackson got stuck behind a red light, which meant I'd get to the house before he did. A few minutes shouldn't make much difference.

As I drove, my thoughts continued to race through everything that had happened.

I didn't think my brain would be able to rest until I had some answers.

When I was only ten minutes away from Phoebe's, her name popped up on the screen on my car dash.

I always felt better after talking to my friend. Maybe she would have some insight on this situation now.

"Where have you been?" I started. "I've been trying to call you back. That must be some dog you're taking care of."

"Joey . . ." Her voice quivered.

Instantly, my blood went cold. I knew there was more to this.

I gripped my wheel tighter. "What's wrong?"

"This job . . . it wasn't what I thought. You've got to help me."

THIRTY-FIVE

"WHAT'S HAPPENING?" I asked Phoebe as my pulse quickened and my grip on the steering wheel tightened even more. "Where are you?"

"I'm at the dog owner's house. When I got here, I went looking for some extra poop bags for Pete. I opened a closet and saw a gun in the closet."

"A gun isn't all that abnormal," I reminded her.

"Did I say gun? I meant guns. Plural. As in, a lot of them. Probably ten or fifteen."

My eyes widened. "That's a lot of guns."

"I know. It's especially a lot of guns to bring on vacation with you. That's when I tried to call you. I needed to know if I was overthinking things."

"I'm so sorry. I was talking to the FBI and couldn't answer."

"Then Pete's dad returned early. I don't think he knew I was here. I had parked across the street because traffic was so backed up. In fact, I was in the bathroom when he came in."

"What happened?"

"He was with someone—someone with an accent."

My lungs froze. "A Russian accent?"

"Maybe."

I could hardly breathe at her words, but I forced air into my lungs anyway. "Phoebe, are you okay?"

"When I noticed they were arguing, I hid out in the bathroom. I thought it would be awkward to step into the middle of it. But they were talking about some really weird stuff."

I stared at the dark beach road ahead as anticipation grew inside me. "Like what?"

"Something about making someone pay. They said this was just the start. That death wasn't enough. I heard them walking closer, so I slipped into the bathroom linen closet. At that point, I was terrified."

"I can only imagine."

"Neither of them came into the bathroom. I heard them leave—but then I realized the closet door was stuck. I can't get out of here!"

"Did you call the police?"

"Of course! But they're not here yet, and I'm

afraid if I hear footsteps, it's going to be these men instead of the cops."

"Just hold tight," I murmured as I pulled into the driveway. "I'll call Jackson and let him know. You're going to be just fine, Phoebe."

"I don't know what's going on." Her voice trembled.

"I don't either, but the picture is becoming a little clearer." I threw my car in Park. "I'll call Jackson now."

"Thanks, Joey."

I got out and, as I scrambled toward Phoebe's house, I dialed his number.

As the phone rang, I heard someone shuffle beside me.

Before I could turn, something zapped my skin.

An electric pulse filled me.

A taser, I realized. I was being tasered.

My phone slipped from my hands.

I dropped to the ground, my limbs trembling.

Everything in my body revolted.

This is nothing like I'd imagined a taser would feel like.

Not that I'd ever wanted to find out.

When I looked up, I saw the man who'd met with Fake Joey.

The one who'd driven away with her in that red sports car.

The look in his eyes was nothing short of malicious.

I was vaguely aware of seeing Fake Joey grinning as she stepped from the shadows beneath the house. Of feeling the man jerk me to my feet and haul me up the stairs into Phoebe's house.

My legs didn't want to cooperate.

It didn't matter. The man practically carried me.

Where was Ripley? Why wasn't he barking?

I didn't know. But I was worried about the dog.

Ripley had always been protective of me.

He'd never let these guys get away with this.

Not if he could help it.

I wanted to call out to him.

But I couldn't talk. I couldn't move.

All I could do was let them do with me whatever they were going to do.

I was stunned. This could not be happening.

But it was.

Jackson couldn't be far behind me.

Unless . . . they'd gotten to him too.

"I'm sorry it had to come down to this," Fake Joey said.

I had a hard time believing that right now.

The woman was even dressed like me.

She wasn't sorry at all.

Without discussing anything, without hesitation, they pushed me inside and dragged me into the guest bathroom off the living room, almost as if they'd planned every last detail. As if they knew the layout of this place and exactly what they wanted to do.

Apparently, they had me exactly where they wanted me just in time because I heard a car pull up outside.

Jackson.

I had to warn him.

If only I could scream.

But I couldn't.

There had to be something I could do.

Before I could even think of a way, the guy put a rag over my mouth and tied it around my head so tightly I nearly squealed with pain.

Then he did the same with my hands. He pulled my arms behind me and wrapped my wrists together.

I was going to be sore from this. If I survived, that is.

The man stayed in the room with me and whispered in my ear, "Don't think of doing anything. You'll regret it. Believe me."

I knew by the tone of his voice that he meant his words.

"Now the real fun begins," Fake Joey said with a smirk.

As she stepped out of the room, I noticed the woman even had her hair and makeup done the same way as mine.

The imposter.

Exactly what was she planning?

Did it have something to do with Jackson?

My heart leapt into my throat.

"I mean it," the man whispered in my ear, his Cheeto-scented breath making me nauseous. "Don't make a move."

It was as if he was reading my mind because I'd briefly considered doing the baloney move on him.

Instead, I gave him my best Raven Remington stink eye.

A moment later, I heard the front door open.

I listened as Jackson dropped his keys on a nearby table, just like he always did.

Then I heard him say, "No problems getting home?"

My heart beat harder. Why was he talking to me as if he could see me?

Then I knew.

My heart sank.

He *did* think he was seeing me.

As if to torture me more, my captor cracked the door open just enough for me to see what was going down.

Fake Joey stood at the window with her back toward Jackson, creating a silhouette.

That was her first mistake. I would never turn my back on Jackson.

But would he notice?

Jackson walked up to her and slid his arms around her waist before nestling his chin against her shoulder. "I don't know about you, but I'm ready for this craziness to be over."

I wanted to struggle against the man holding me. To yell out.

But I could do neither of those things.

I would kick something to make a noise, but I still felt weak from the taser.

If there's one thing I hate, it's feeling helpless.

What exactly was she planning?

The next instant, Jackson jerked his hands away from Fake Joey and stepped back.

He reached for his gun.

Before he could grab it, Fake Joey drew her own gun and pointed it at his chest. "I wouldn't do that, cowboy."

I HAD no idea what was about to play out.

But the next moment, my captor threw the bathroom door open and stepped out, shoving me in front of him.

I nearly toppled forward, but he grabbed my arms to hold me up upright.

Pain traveled through me. My arms weren't supposed to bend that way.

I didn't think I'd broken anything, but man did that hurt. Thank goodness, I had a stunt double on *Relentless*.

Jackson's eyes met mine, and I saw the worry there.

"You don't need to do anything rash," Jackson said with a calm voice.

"That's what they all say," Fake Joey said. "Keep your hands up."

Her voice had changed. No longer was it friendly and cheerful. Now, it was hardened with a slight country drawl.

Her mannerisms had also transformed, no longer matching mine. Instead, her posture was stiff.

Any moment, I expected her to pull her face off and reveal somebody else.

But that part didn't happen.

Not yet.

"I need you to put your gun on the floor and push it toward me. Slowly," Fake Joey said. "One wrong move, and she'll die. Not even kidding."

"Okay . . ." Jackson slowly took his gun from his holster, set it on the floor, and used his foot to push it toward her. "What do you want from us?"

"Everything." Her eyes gleamed with greed. "I want everything."

A chill went through me. This woman didn't only want to impersonate me. She wanted to *be* me.

My blood nearly froze at the thought.

There was only one way she could do that.

Over my dead body.

The man jerked the fabric from around my mouth. I ran my tongue across the top of my lips, trying to get rid of the dryness.

"We just need to talk this through," I finally croaked. "Starting with . . . who are you?"

Fake Joey stepped closer to me, an empty look in her eyes. "You really don't know?"

"I don't."

"You're such a disappointment. I thought you would've figured it out by now. My name is Priscilla Covington." She paused, watching my expression. "What? You don't recognize it?"

"I'm afraid I don't." I was fairly certain I'd never heard that name before.

"I'm your half-sister, you moron," she announced.

I reeled as my thoughts pummeled me.

"I have a sister?" What sense did that make?

My dad didn't have any more kids. He would have told me.

Unless my dad wasn't really my dad.

A sick feeling swirled in my stomach.

"I see the shock all over your face." Fake Joey paused in front of me. "So you really didn't know I existed, did you?"

The man behind me had his gun trained on Jackson while Fake Joey—or should I call her Priscilla now?—swung hers all over the place haphazardly.

"I didn't know you existed either. I didn't know I had any family until I went searching for answers when I turned sixteen," Priscilla said. "Did you know we were born only eight months apart? That's right. Our dad was a very busy man. You're older, by the way."

"Wait . . . you're saying that the man who's claiming to be my dad is also your dad, which makes us half-sisters?" Numbness filled me as I asked the question.

"I always knew you were a bright one." She stared at me mockingly.

I might have scowled, but this didn't seem like the time for it.

"So, anyway, I saw you on TV. You looked so much like me . . . I got curious and went looking for answers. Found my mom. Found out my dad's name. Adolf, of all names. Horrible, right?"

We could agree on that, at least.

"Then I did one of those DNA tests that you mail in to find out your heritage."

Facts began clicking in place. I'd done one of those once also, but I'd never followed up. I think I'd gotten a role in a movie and had pretty much forgotten about it. "Is that right?"

"They connected me with you. That's when my bio mom said she knew about you. I couldn't help but think about how differently our lives had turned out."

"Why didn't you just come find me?" I asked. "We could've—"

"We could've what? Had a nice family reunion?" Her eyes narrowed again. "Truth is, I thought about it several times. But then I thought about what a great life you had while my life had been so horrible. A movie star half-sister? Really? You had a dad who raised you. Loved you. While I got dumped with the county. I seriously went from foster home to foster home, and I experienced terrible things."

"I'm so sorry . . . I didn't know. I mean, I had no idea."

She ignored me. "So I started working in Hollywood, thinking if it was good for you, maybe it would be good for me. I mean, how hard can it be, right? Pretending to be someone you're not? Even though I was a pretty good actress, I couldn't pay the bills that way. Instead, I became a makeup artist."

"So you're using makeup to look like me?"

She shrugged. "We're half-sisters, not twins. That would make things too easy now, wouldn't it? It doesn't matter. I know how to contour makeup to make my face look different. If I were to take all my makeup off right now, I wouldn't look as much like you."

"You're very good at what you do." Maybe if I complimented her, she might like me a little bit more right now.

"Once I figured out that I could look like you, then I realized I could imitate you. Then I realized just how much more I could really do with it."

I sucked in a breath.

I didn't like the sound of that.

CHAPTER
THIRTY-SEVEN

"I STILL DON'T KNOW what your angle is now," I said before stealing a glance at Jackson.

Did she really think she could become me? Was that what she wanted?

She was living in a fantasy land. I may be an actress, but that didn't mean I didn't have any real-life troubles.

In fact, I have my fair share of them.

Look at this situation I'm in right now . . . . I couldn't even make this up if I tried.

Jackson seemed to be listening with rapt attention, poised to make a move if he had to. But these guys had guns, and we didn't. Jackson's gun was still on the floor just out of reach.

Was there a chance he could dive for it? If he

could just get his hands on a weapon, I know he could take down these two in three seconds flat.

"I discovered I could use my skills and makeup to do things," Priscilla continued. "I could disguise myself. Then Benny and I started taking things that didn't belong to us."

Benny. That was the name of this guy behind me. I wasn't sure if he and Priscilla were romantically linked or business partners. Maybe they were both.

"Taking things? You mean like artwork?"

She grinned. "Now you're catching on. I met Benny in LA. He's an amazing artist—especially when it comes to imitating masterpieces. We were both struggling. That's when we came up with a plan."

An artist? Had that been red paint on his sleeve when I saw him behind the coffee shop—not blood?

My eyes narrowed as my thoughts continued to swirl. "But what about that conversation I heard you having behind the grocery store?"

Her eyebrows shot up. "You heard that? I guess it doesn't matter anymore. I knew I only had a few days to convince people I was you. All my public appearances were just trial runs."

"But he handed you something."

"You mean the backup jump drive so I could save my social media posts?"

Well, that was a bit of a letdown.

"And you mentioned three days." I studied her face.

"Yes. There were three days until the museum opened." Priscilla rolled her eyes as if annoyed. "Anyway . . . when I heard about the opening of the museum and that you were going to be a part of it, I knew exactly what I needed to do. I just didn't expect to enjoy impersonating you so much. I figured while I was at it, I would try to make your life miserable. After all, I shouldn't be the sister with all the sob stories."

"I know my life might look perfect on the outside, but it's anything but. I've had a lot of my own struggles, Priscilla. Just because I haven't posted them all over the internet doesn't mean they haven't happened."

"I'm not in the mood to feel any sympathy for you right now." She raised her nose in the air as if she didn't believe me. "But then things got better. It was like something in my life was finally working in my favor when Dad showed up here in Nags Head."

I still refused to believe that Adolf was actually my dad. But this wasn't the time to think that through. I had to concentrate on survival first.

"Are you the one who abducted him?" I asked.

A flicker of surprise passed her gaze. "Abducted him?"

She really didn't know about that, did she? Which meant she hadn't done it.

But if not Priscilla, then who?

How was this all connected?

I now had the answers as to who Fake Joey was— or at least who she claimed to be. I knew how she was connected to the art theft.

But nothing else made sense.

Suddenly, I heard someone burst through the door behind me.

I hoped it was the police arriving to save us.

Then I saw my fake Dad . . . along with two other men, who were holding guns.

The two men with Adolf weren't working with him, I realized.

They were holding Fake Dad captive.

I quickly observed Adolf. He had a black eye. A busted lip. He appeared hunched.

They'd given him a good beating, hadn't they?

My heart panged when I saw how painful it looked.

At once, Priscilla's and Benny's guns went to the men while the men aimed their guns at them.

I stood at the intersection of all the barrels.

"Joey . . ." Fake Dad stared at me. "You're okay."

"I think everyone just needs to take a step back here," Jackson said.

"We need you to come with us," one of the men with Fake Dad—the tall one—said as he nodded toward me.

Wouldn't you know . . . the guy had a Russian accent?

I knew going anywhere with anyone at this point would be a very bad idea.

Most likely, I'd never be seen alive again if that happened.

We'd covered that statistic in more than one episode of *Relentless*.

"What do you want from me?" I asked, still realizing that if anyone pulled the trigger, I would be the most likely one to get hurt here.

"We need you as leverage," Tall Russian said.

"Leverage for what?" I blurted.

"Joey . . ." Fake Dad looked at me. "You don't want to mess with these guys."

"We just need you to come," Stocky Russian said.

Priscilla stepped forward, her motions thick with

attitude. "She's my sister. You're not taking her. But you can do whatever you want to with my dad."

Fake Dad looked at her in shock until his expression seemed to crumple. "What?"

"That's right. Do you remember Amy Covington?"

"Amy? I haven't heard her name in years."

"I'm her kid. She told me you were my father—after I tracked her down and asked. But she said you didn't want me, just like she didn't want me. Then I was just tossed away to the fringes of society to become what I am today. I obviously got some of your skills though, didn't I? Crime seems to come naturally to me."

"The fact that you were born . . . I never knew."

"That's right. You never knew. Because you left mom, and she went a little crazy. And I was the one who had to pay the consequences."

"If I could go back and do things over again . . ." Adolf's gaze appeared strained with grief.

"But you can't!" Priscilla practically spit as she said the words. "What's done is done. Now it's brought us to this point."

"Enough talking!" Stocky Russian said. "Joey Darling, come with us."

He nodded to Tall Russian, and the man stepped toward me.

Jackson jerked forward, grabbed me and pulled me back.

All the guns swiveled toward him.

"She's not going anywhere with you," Jackson announced.

"We'll put a bullet through your head if that's what we have to do to get to her," Tall Russian said.

"What did that guy do to you?" Jackson nodded at Fake Dad.

"Stabbed us in the back," the man said. "He stole sensitive Russian intel, and we need to make an example of him. Death was too easy. So we had to find someone he cared about to use as leverage. It's your lucky day, Joey Darling."

I wasn't feeling very lucky.

"How does Sasha fit into this?" I asked, trying to buy some time.

"We wanted to find out more information on you. Danny seemed like an easy target. We were right. Although she didn't find anything useful in your house. I figured it was worth it to shake you up."

"Which one of you is Pete's owner?" I asked.

"Who's Pete?" Jackson muttered. "These guys own someone?"

"Pete is the dog Phoebe's dog-sitting," I whispered.

"Pete's mine," Tall Russian said.

"You're not a photographer. That was surveillance equipment. And being around her was just another way to find out information about me, wasn't it?"

Tall Russian pointed to his temple. "Smart woman."

As I stared at the danger all around us, I realized I had no idea how Jackson and I would get out of this situation.

ONE OF FAKE Dad's abductors tried to grab me again, but Jackson wedged himself in front of me.

Then Priscilla also nudged herself in front of me.

But it wasn't to protect me.

It was because she was determined to get her way.

Under other circumstances, I might feel honored, having so many people fighting over who gets me.

Not so much in this case.

"You can't have her," Fake Joey sneered like a possessive dog fighting over a bone. "She's mine."

"What's that mean?" Fake Dad squinted in confusion.

I had to think it took a lot to confuse a spy. But Fake Joey was just messed up enough to do the job.

"I'm going to become Joey Darling. I know her lines. Her movies. Everything about her life. It's going to be my greatest con yet."

"You're going to kill her?" Fake Dad blinked as if in shock.

Priscilla chuckled. "I can't really justify killing the only sister that I have. I was kind of hoping we might be BFFs one day, and that would be kind of hard if she was dead. But I have a few plans of how I can take her out of the limelight."

"Like what?" I couldn't keep the incredulous tone from my voice.

"For starters, I stole your birth certificate," she said.

"That was you?"

She smirked again. "I decided to explore your house, you know, get to know you better. That's when I discovered it. I figured that would come in handy."

"But it still wouldn't get me out of the picture."

"I have plans of framing you for all my past crimes."

"But the police will check our fingerprints! They won't match." There was no way she'd get away with this.

She scowled this time. "I'll figure that out. In the

meantime, I'm going to take you somewhere no one will find you. Maybe once I have all your money, I'll buy a nice cabin in the middle of nowhere. I'll let you live there—in the basement or something. That way we can be besties. Then I'll step into your life, and no one will ever know. If you try to escape, you'll end up in prison."

A shiver rushed down my spine.

That sounded horrific.

I wanted to tell her she was insane, but I didn't think that would help matters any.

I swallowed hard before asking, "And Jackson?"

She shrugged as if he were an afterthought. "It only makes sense to eliminate him."

Her story had so many holes in it, but I wasn't sure pointing that out would be the right thing.

"This whole conversation is ridiculous!" Stocky Russian said. "Enough talking. We need to get her, and we need to go."

I tensed. This was it. The moment my future hinged on.

I closed my eyes and lifted a prayer.

Then I heard glass shatter, followed by gunfire.

I expected to feel pain. To fall to my knees. To draw my last breath.

Instead, Tall Russian fell to the floor.

As he did, Benny pulled the trigger.

But instead of hitting the other Russian, his bullet grazed Fake Joey's arm.

She yelped and dropped her gun.

Wait. Had Benny shot at Fake Joey on purpose? Or had he been aiming for Stocky Russian and missed?

The jury was still out.

As Fake Joey's gun skittered across the floor, Jackson grabbed it.

But not before Stocky Russian shot Benny, who then fell to the floor with a moan.

I knew what was about to happen next.

Stocky Russian would go for Jackson.

And I couldn't let that happen.

"Don't even think about it." I said as Stocky Russian aimed at Jackson. Seeing Jackson in the line of danger suddenly reenergized me. It was as if I'd never been tased.

I turned, kicked him just below his knee, and yelled, "Baloney."

My signature move that my real dad had taught me in real life. It had come in handy on several occasions.

Stocky Russian guy yelped in pain and dropped his gun.

Jackson started to step toward the guy.

Just then, Tall Russian climbed to his feet. Blood gushing from the bullet wound on his shoulder.

I held my breath as I waited to see what would happen.

"The smart thing would be to leave right now," Jackson said.

"I can't do that," Tall Russian said. "Not until I have what's fully mine."

"Your issue isn't with Joey, so leave her out of this."

"I'm afraid it doesn't work that way." The man sneered.

Jackson's finger poised over the trigger. "Yes, it does."

Another bullet sliced through the air.

Again, I wasn't sure where it came from—only that it flew from behind me, from outside the broken window.

I waited again, unsure what had happened.

Then Tall Russian assassin dropped to the floor. Again.

Judging by the look of his chest wound, this time I didn't think he'd be getting back up.

Jackson loosened his muscles as he glanced at me.

"You didn't fire that did you?" I asked.

"No, I didn't." Jackson grabbed the gun Stocky Russian had dropped when I'd kicked him, and then he ran to the window and looked out.

I followed behind him and saw a lithe figure hop into a car and pull away.

My mom.

Again.

She just ambushed the Russians, saved me, and left, just like she'd done the last time I had seen her.

I suppose I should be grateful.

I would tell her as much if she'd stick around long enough for me to talk to her.

Instead, I turned back to Fake Dad. Then I looked at Fake Joey as she lay on the floor crying and holding her arm.

One Russian assassin sprawled lifeless. The other writhed in pain as he sat on the floor holding his knee.

I think with all the practice I've gotten with my baloney move, I've gotten pretty good at it.

I could hardly wait to tell my real dad next time I saw him.

For now, I looked at Fake Dad again, not even sure where to start.

But I didn't have to.

Because sirens surrounded us as SUVs with

flashing lights screamed up to the house, and the FBI flooded inside.

Maybe this was over.

I finally had some answers.

But did I have enough?

THIRTY MINUTES LATER, arrests had been made.

The assassins had been taken away, one in handcuffs and the other in the coroner's vehicle.

Benny had also been handcuffed and put in the back of an ambulance.

Ripley had been found locked in a neighbor's outdoor shower area—and he was okay.

Before the FBI took Fake Joey to the police station, I asked for a few minutes. I had a couple of things I wanted to say to her.

Did I really have a sister? I mean, that would explain why the two of us looked so much alike.

But if I acknowledged that then I'd also be acknowledging that my dad wasn't really my dad and this Adolf man was.

I wasn't sure I could stomach that right now.

I already felt like my world had been turned upside down.

This whole thing should be an episode of *Relentless* or a Hollywood blockbuster. It wasn't something that should happen to me in real life.

I wondered how long it would take for me to come to terms with this.

"It didn't have to be this way," I started as I turned to Priscilla.

She scowled and glanced at the bandage covering her bicep. She appeared as if she wanted to touch it, but her handcuffs prevented her from doing so. "Sure, it did."

"You should have just talked to me." I wasn't going to justify anything she said.

"You wouldn't have given me the time of the day." Her eyes narrowed as she looked away bitterly.

"You don't know that." She'd made a lot of assumptions in this whole process.

"It doesn't matter. What's done is done now. I've messed up my life royally while you get off scot-free. Heck, you'll probably somehow profit off this. Turn it into a best-selling book or something."

I ignored the comment—even though it was a decent idea. "It's never too late to turn things around."

I wasn't sure where those words came from. Except that I knew I lived them myself. I was constantly in the process of trying to turn my life around. To let go of the old me and to improve the new me.

And sometimes I failed.

Like in the case of Danny.

Sad thing was, it didn't appear that Priscilla was even willing to consider changing. I knew I couldn't change her. If she wanted to be a better person, it had to be her doing.

After FBI agents hauled Priscilla away, Jackson pulled me into his arms.

"That was close," he muttered.

"Yes, it was." Too close, in my opinion.

"I have good news. Officer Byron was able to find Phoebe in the closet and release her. She's shaken but fine."

Relief swept through me. "I'm so glad to hear that."

"We both are."

"Where is she now?"

"Heading to the police station to give her statement. One of her friends from work offered her a place to stay tonight since Phoebe's house is now a crime scene. She agreed to spend the night."

"Smart thinking." I was so glad she was okay.

"Also, right before I came into the house, I heard back from our CSI tech. That photo we found of you and Fake Dad *was* photoshopped."

"What?"

"My guess is that Fake Joey left it in hopes of messing with your head."

Had I ever used a photo of me with Bunny-Boo for an interview? I wasn't sure. I had given my manager a stack of old photos once. Maybe that's where Fake Joey had gotten the original picture. Then she'd found a picture of Adolf, and she'd let some creative magic happen.

I frowned. The lengths Priscilla had gone through . . . Her actions actually made me sad more than anything else.

She'd been given a bad hand in life. Instead of trying to turn it around in a healthy manner, she'd let bitterness take over.

I released a breath and then asked, "And what about Sasha?"

"When she ran from the smoothie shop, Danny realized something was up. He reported her to the chief. She was found trying to escape the OBX, but officers caught her."

"Wow." That was a lot to process.

But there was still more weighing on my mind.

"That was my mom who fired those shots from outside."

His jaw tightened. "I know."

"I don't even know what to think about this."

"You probably won't know for a while. You have to give yourself time to process this and to find out some answers."

"I still don't understand why these guys that were after Fake Dad were doing drive-by shootings."

"They were trying to make it look random. At first, they wanted to take him out. Then they realized they wanted to make him suffer first. That's why they started coming after you."

I was going to have to wait to talk to him, to try to figure out answers.

But I didn't want to hear answers from him.

I wanted to hear answers from my *dad* dad. I wanted him to reassure me that he really was my father and that everything would be okay—just like he used to do when I was little.

How I longed sometimes to go back to the simplicity of those days, when I knew I didn't have to worry because my dad did all the worrying for me.

At least, some of my worries could be put to rest for now.

The next morning, I was finally able to talk to Adolf.

The FBI had let him go.

I'd called him and invited him to my house. Jackson would be here, but he promised to stay in the other room—close enough to jump in if I needed him, but far enough away to give us a little privacy.

I'd be lying if I didn't admit I was nervous. Because I was.

But maybe I could finally get some answers.

Jackson and I had stayed at our house last night. Our new window replacement was on its way, so soon I wouldn't be able to tell anything had happened.

Maybe my life would return to normal.

On second thought, was my life ever really normal?

Not really.

I heard a car pull into the driveway, and I glanced out the window.

It was Adolf.

"You've got this," Jackson murmured as he squeezed my shoulder.

"Thanks."

He kissed my forehead before we walked together toward the door. We ushered Adolf inside.

Jackson stepped away, and the two of us took a seat in the living room.

Awkwardness stretched through the room.

Adolf looked up at me, an almost apologetic look in his burdened eyes. He had stitches at his temple, his eye was still black, and he had a sling on his arm.

"I never wanted things to happen this way," he stated, his wrinkles seeming to deepen.

"I know." Deep inside, I did believe that was true. "Have you known about me since I was born?"

I would talk as if I was his daughter—but I wasn't fully convinced yet.

He nodded. "I have. I figured you were better off without me. And Lew seemed to be a great dad."

"And Priscilla?"

"I had no idea about her. Amy and I . . . we were just a fling."

I studied his face. "So, let me get this story straight. You stole some intel from Russia in your time as a spy, and then Russian operatives came and tracked you down."

"That's right."

"Originally, they wanted to kill you, but they changed their minds and decided to make you suffer instead. One of those ways they could make you suffer was by making me suffer. That's why they showed up at my place."

"Also correct."

I let out a sigh. I didn't know what to think about all of this.

"I heard you went off grid," I finally said. "Does that mean you've turned your back on our country?"

He shook his head, still appearing solemn. "Not at all. I had to go into hiding so these guys wouldn't find me."

"But you came here looking for me?"

"No one else knew about you but me. I figured it was safe as long as I used an alias for my last name. But they must have followed me." He paused before leaning closer. "I know it's going to take you some time to process this."

"To say the least."

"I hope when this is over, maybe we could . . . be friends? I don't expect to be your dad, Joey. I missed that train. But I'd love to get to know you."

"I'll think about it," I told him, unwilling to commit to anything.

First, I wanted to check his DNA test to make sure I wasn't being scammed. The results weren't back yet.

Finally, I stood, knowing there were other things I needed to take care of.

He stepped toward the door and offered a wave.

I had his number. If I called, would he answer?

Or would he be on some type of top-secret assignment overseas?

I didn't know.

Maybe I'd find out.

Maybe I wouldn't.

As Adolf pulled away, I spotted MaryAnn emerge from her sensible silver Corolla, which had appeared in the driveway. I stepped out to meet her.

When she spotted me, I stopped in my tracks as more guilt filled me.

"I thought I might find you here." She paused in front of me on the sidewalk.

"You're looking for me?" I wasn't sure I liked the sound of that.

MaryAnn was a sweet, gentle soul . . . but sweet, gentle souls could still want revenge.

However, the most heinous thing I could see her doing was knitting me a hot pad in the shape of a broken heart.

"That's right." She frowned. "I'm still not happy about what you did to my Danny."

"I know. And, again, I'm so sorry—"

She held up a hand to stop me from any more blathering. "No more apologies. I have to admit, however, that maybe being a cop isn't suited for him. Nor was marriage. Sasha is already gone, and I couldn't be happier about that. Apparently, the marriage won't stick since a license wasn't filed with the county."

I didn't tell her that the woman had been arrested. The old Joey would have. The new Joey would be more tight-lipped.

"That's good news, I guess," I said instead.

"Danny just took a job as a security guard at the water park down the street."

I raised my eyebrows. "Really? But he was only on temporary suspension."

"He decided leaving the force was the best option. At least, he won't be handling any top-secret information that way. Plus, he should be a little safer doing that."

"It sounds like it could be a win-win for him then."

"That's what I'm hoping. I just wanted to stop by and tell you that there are no hard feelings. Okay?"

"That means a lot to me, MaryAnn. Thank you."

She gave me a hug before leaving.

Jackson and Ripley joined me outside. He glanced at his watch. "Only an hour until Amanda shows up."

Yes, I'd called Amanda.

I'd decided that I definitely needed to tell people about what had happened. Who knew what else Fake Joey had done? I needed to set the record straight, and Amanda had agreed that I could approve the story before it went live. Actually, my manager had her sign an official agreement so there would be no more slipups.

Her cameraman had apparently filmed me as I watched that video of Fake Joey outside of Beach Combers after the shooting. They asked if they could play that on air, and I'd agreed.

I'd decided I wouldn't mention Adolf during the interview. I wanted to keep that part of my life quiet.

But sometimes keeping secrets wasn't the best policy. Sometimes being transparent was the way to go.

Priscilla, for example. If she'd just talked to me, we could have avoided so much of this drama.

I turned toward Jackson. "All of this seems surreal."

"Yes, it does."

"The good news is that Phoebe now has a new dog."

Yes, Phoebe was going to take Pete since his owner had been killed.

I glanced down at Ripley and rubbed his head.

"You're going to have a new friend. Aren't you excited?"

Ripley barked and wagged his tail.

"The other good news is that we recovered the lighthouse painting in the back of Priscilla's car," Jackson said. "The museum is back on track to open —only a couple of days late."

"Is that why Don keeps calling me?"

Jackson smiled. "Probably. However, don't be surprised if he tells you you're no longer invited to help."

I let out a laugh. I wouldn't blame him.

I pulled my arms more tightly around Jackson and nestled my head into his chest. "Thank you for always being there for me."

"Of course. That's what I'm supposed to do."

"But you do it so well."

He shrugged. "When you love someone, you don't want it any other way."

I rested in his embrace.

Yes, when you loved someone, you'd do anything to protect them.

I only hoped my loved ones would say the same about me. I'd do anything to protect them also—even if my methods were sometimes less than conventional and marred with mistakes.

I didn't want anything to happen to the people I loved. Not on my watch, at least.

My thoughts turned to my father, and I frowned.

I prayed I could protect him throughout whatever the future held also. I still had no idea why Frank thought my dad knew something before he'd disappeared the second time.

Had Frank read too much into things? Or was there more to this story than I realized?

But in the meantime, I would treasure each moment with Jackson and Ripley.

~~~

Thank you so much for reading *Not on My Botch*. If you enjoyed this book, please consider leaving a review!

Next book in the series coming soon: *One Hit Blunder*
~~~

COMING SOON

ALSO BY CHRISTY BARRITT:

THE WORST DETECTIVE EVER

I'm not really a private detective. I just play one on TV.

Joey Darling, better known to the world as Raven Remington, detective extraordinaire, is trying to separate herself from her invincible alter ego. She played the spunky character for five years on the hit TV show *Relentless*, which catapulted her to fame and into the role of Hollywood's sweetheart. When her marriage falls apart, her finances dwindle to nothing, and her father disappears, Joey finds herself on the Outer Banks of North Carolina, trying to piece together her life away from the limelight. But as people continually mistake her for the character she played on TV, she's tasked with solving real life crimes . . . even though she's terrible at it.

ABOUT THE AUTHOR

USA Today has called Christy Barritt's books "scary, funny, passionate, and quirky."

Christy writes both mystery and romantic suspense novels that are clean with underlying messages of faith. Her books have sold more than three million copies and have won the Daphne du Maurier Award for Excellence in Suspense and Mystery, have been twice nominated for the Romantic Times Reviewers' Choice Award, and have finaled for both a Carol Award and Foreword Magazine's Book of the Year.

She is married to her Prince Charming, a man who thinks she's hilarious—but only when she's not trying to be. Christy is a self-proclaimed klutz, an avid music lover who's known for spontaneously bursting into song, and a road trip aficionado.

When she's not working or spending time with her family, she enjoys singing, playing the guitar, and exploring small, unsuspecting towns where people have no idea how accident-prone she is.

Find Christy online at:
www.christybarritt.com
www.facebook.com/christybarritt
www.twitter.com/cbarritt

Sign up for Christy's newsletter to get information on all of her latest releases here: **www.christybarritt. com/newsletter-sign-up/**

facebook.com / AuthorChristyBarritt
twitter.com / christybarritt
instagram.com / cebarritt